PENGUIN ⦿ CLASSICS

WORKS AND DAYS

HESIOD probably lived and composed in the late eighth century BCE in the hamlet of Askra in Boeotia, mainland Greece. Alongside the works of Homer, his poems mark the beginning of Western literature. The first Western poet to give his own biography, Hesiod describes himself as a farmer, son of an Asia Minor sea merchant, and winner of the Amphidamas' funeral games tripod in poetry.

A. E. STALLINGS is an American poet and translator who lives in Greece. She has published three books of poetry, *Archaic Smile* (1999), *Hapax* (2006) and *Olives* (2012); another, *Like*, is forthcoming. She has received fellowships from the Guggenheim and MacArthur Foundations. Her verse translation of Lucretius' *The Nature of Things* (2007) is published in Penguin Classics.

T0201139

HESIOD

Works and Days

Translated and with an Introduction and Notes by
A. E. STALLINGS

PENGUIN BOOKS

PENGUIN CLASSICS

UK | USA | Canada | Ireland | Australia
India | New Zealand | South Africa

Penguin Books is part of the Penguin Random House group of companies
whose addresses can be found at global.penguinrandomhouse.com

This edition first published in Penguin Classics 2018

007

Translation and editorial material © A. E. Stallings, 2018
All rights reserved

The moral rights of the editor and translator have been asserted

Set in 11.25/14 pt Sabon LT Std
Typeset by Jouve (UK), Milton Keynes
Printed and bound in Great Britain by Clays Ltd, Elcograf S.p.A.

ISBN: 978–0–141–19752–4

Contents

WORKS AND DAYS

Introduction

A Nugget of Irritation

From where we stand, the poems of Hesiod, alongside the Homeric epics, the *Iliad* and the *Odyssey*, emerge at the rosy dawn of Western literature, yet also at the sunset of a purely oral tradition we can only glimpse in reflective glow. Who Homer was – he, she, or they – no one will ever know, and conjecture scarcely alters how we read and are affected by those masterpieces. But Hesiod presents himself in his poems as an individual personality, as a self-proclaimed poet. The personality is intrinsic to the poems, particularly to *Works and Days*, the occasion for which was, at least if we take Hesiod's word for it, a dispute between the author and his brother over the division of a paternal inheritance.

Around this nugget of irritation, Hesiod fashions a variegated and discursive poem about justice and man's place in the world, addressing these themes through an assortment of strategies: myth, allegory, personal asides, philosophy, theology, Old-Testament-prophet-style rants on the world's going to hell in a hand-basket, lyrical descriptions of the natural world, astronomy, homespun proverbs, phenology (the science of watching nature for first signs of the changing seasons), an almanac of the farmer's yearly round of tasks, and a calendar of lucky and unlucky days. Possibly the poem continued past where it ends now, to include a section on the reading of bird omens. Didactic epics in the centuries to follow (Virgil's *Georgics*, for instance) nod to Hesiod as the genre's pioneer, but there is nothing else in the canon quite like *Works and Days*, with its quirky mix of the cosmic, the earthy and the personal. For the ancients, the adjective for Homer's high epic style was 'sublime', while the word for Hesiod's sure command of the middle style was 'sweetness'.

Homer may be as old or older than Hesiod (the question is itself ancient), but can hardly be described as a personality or having an individual voice – the essence of epic sublimity is to eschew one – and the biographies that attach to the name are various and conflicting. Hesiod, the first self-styled poet in Western literature, the first to tell us his own name and provide us with his own 'bio', is also the first to advertise himself as a prize-winning poet: winner of a tripod (a three-legged cauldron) at the poetry competition at a funeral games on the island of Euboea. In fact Hesiod presents himself in the earlier *Theogony* as having received his laurels (a bay staff rather than a wreath) directly from the Muses while pasturing his flock on the slopes of Mount Helikon: thus a poet laureate. Poetry has changed a lot in the intervening millennia. Poets, not so much.

Hesiod probably composed the *Theogony* and *Works and Days* sometime in the last third of the eighth century or at the cusp of the seventh (700 BCE); other poems apocryphally ascribed to him, such as *The Catalogue of Women*, a continuation of the *Theogony* of which we only have fragments, and *The Shield of Hercules*, are probably of a later date. Contrary to general perceptions of ancient Greek history, which focus on the glories of the classical period (the fifth and fourth centuries BCE), the eighth century was a vibrant period for Greece. The first Olympics, for instance, is traditionally dated to 776 BCE. Greece was emerging from the Greek Dark Ages,[1] into a time of active trade and travel across the Mediterranean, an expansion of Greek settlements along coasts to the east in Asia Minor (indeed into the Black Sea) and to the west in Sicily and Italy, and as far as France and Spain. Trade, travel, and exchange exposed Greece to 'Orientalizing' influences from Mesopotamia, the Phoenicians, and Egypt, and the Greek tweaking of a Western Semitic script to include vowels led to the rise of a radical new communication technology, easily learned and transmitted without a scribe's elite and arcane education, and able to record the sounds of speech: the Greek alphabet.[2]

Hesiod, According to Hesiod

Hesiod was born in mainland Greece, if we take his single sea-journey claim at face value. By his own account, he seems to be a farmer from a village, Askra, in the mainland Greek region of Boeotia. He has a brother, Perses, who is probably younger. There is the suggestion of a fine family pedigree somewhere in the distant past. His father was a merchant sailor from Aeolian Kyme in Asia Minor who, unable to make a decent enough living at it, sailed across the Aegean to mainland Greece, settling in Askra at the foot of Mount Helikon. Presumably it is the father's death that has set in motion the brothers' dispute.

The name 'Hesiod' doesn't appear in *Works and Days*.

Rather Hesiod mentions himself by name only in an ear-
lier poem, the *Theogony* (*Th.* 22), but Hesiod of Askra is
traditionally considered the author of both poems. *Works
and Days* mentions a previous poem (a hymn) by the
poet; there is a strong argument to be made that this is in
fact the *Theogony*.

Ancient commenters disagree about the meaning of
'Hesiod', but one suggestion is that it is Aeolic for 'he
who travels an auspicious road', a hopeful name for a
child of émigrés. In the *Theogony*, Hesiod, with his pen-
chant for etymology as destiny, himself suggests that
his name means 'song-slinger'. 'Perses', the name of his
brother, on the other hand, would seem to mean 'destroyer'
or maybe 'wastrel'.

It is usual to think of Hesiod as a misogynist. I've come
to think of him more as a misanthrope: he isn't any kinder
to men to my mind. His stance towards women in *Works
and Days* seems softened from his attitude in the *Theog-
ony*. In the earlier poem, they are mere mouths to feed
and contribute nothing, and are compared to drones eat-
ing up the honey of the diligent bees. In *Works and Days*
(305),[3] Hesiod uses the same simile instead for work-shy
men. In the *Theogony* Pandora, referred to only as a
'modest maiden', the mother of the deadly tribe of women,
is given to mankind as a punishment. In *Works and Days*,
Pandora, the 'All-endowed', is still given as revenge, a
bane to all bread-earning men. But she isn't un-useful –
Athena teaches her to weave beautiful cloth, for instance.
And she is just part of the punitive package, which also
includes work itself, a curse from which Hesiod fashions a
mixed blessing, a virtue from a necessity. The womb-like
jar pours forth evils, but contains Hope. It's no coinci-
dence that Pandora herself is a vessel made of clay.

I am struck too by Hesiod's unexpected kindliness towards the teenaged girl whom he describes luxuriating in her winter bath (519ff.). You would think this image would stir Hesiod's ire: here she is, another mouth to feed, dawdling in the middle of the day, contributing nothing, using precious unguents on her skin, taking a nap. But the image is rather one of tenderness and affection. It's worth wondering what this scene is even doing set in hardscrabble Askra, whether it isn't some nostalgic paternal (or maternal) memory from Asia Minor.

Perses needs to be warned that a woman in tight skirts is after his barn, but women in *Works and Days* do contribute to the farmstead: a bondswoman follows the oxen in the furrows (she is one of the elements necessary to ward off famine, in fact), and it is helpful to have a serving girl in the house, so long as she doesn't have any kids to distract her. There are lucky days for the conception of girl children, which suggests to me that they were not necessarily unwanted. It is good to marry at the right time, and a man acquires nothing better than a good wife (702).

Hesiod's World, According to Hesiod

Hesiod's woebegone hamlet of Askra was home to, if we go by the occupations mentioned in the poem, a blacksmith, a wainwright/joiner, farmers and their hired labourers, and slaves or serfs.

If we include the four professions Hesiod says are subject to envy, Askra might also have contained builders, potters, beggars, and bards, as well as perhaps the *basilêes*, the authorities called upon to settle disputes. It is unclear whether the marketplace in which Perses loiters looking for trouble and where the 'kings' (perhaps better translated for

Hesiod's time as lords or chieftains, magistrates or judges)[4] assemble, is somehow attached to Askra; more likely this refers to the nearby city of Thespiae, which no doubt held sway over the smaller settlement.

It's a world that does not much resemble the Mycenaean-era cities and kings portrayed in the *Iliad*, but which does have something in common with the Ithakan homestead, more prosperous ranch than palace, in the *Odyssey*. Odysseus' father, Laertes, in his patched shirt and goat-skin cap, working his own farm on the outskirts of town, could be Hesiod's neighbour.

Life in mainland Greece in the late eighth or early seventh century BCE, as Hesiod describes it, is difficult and precarious: the ever-present threat is not war but starvation. The reality of hunger is brought home by the casual mention of a poor man's consolation, mallow and asphodel. (In the famine winter of 1941–2 in modern Greece, the ability to forage, countryside versus city, was sometimes the difference between life and death.) Hesiod and Perses, however, don't appear to be merely subsistence farmers. Hesiod gives his brother advice should he wish to go into their father's former business, merchant shipping. This contributes to the impression of a yeomanry.

What's more, in Hesiod's world there is also time for feasting and religious festivals, for taking a break in the heat of summer to enjoy a jug of wine (imported vintage no less) and loaf of bread in the shade. A farmer doing well for himself might have the means to hire a labourer, and a serving girl in the house, perhaps to spin and weave. He might even have the means to marry. Marriage is double-edged: potentially a bulwark against the troubles of old age (the promise of descendants, and extra farm hands), but incurring the burden of more hungry mouths.

We tend to think of lifespans in the distant past as drastically briefer than our own, but once we factor out infant mortality and childhood ailments, someone who had safely reached puberty might not unreasonably hope to live out the three score and ten years allotted man by the Psalms – eighty, the Psalmist assures us, if in good health. In Hesiod's vigorous world, a forty-year-old labourer is in his prime with none of a young man's flightiness about him, and thirty is about the right age for a man to think of settling down. To be sure, he ought to pick a maiden four years past the onset of puberty; let's say menarche occurs at fourteen or fifteen, maybe later[5] – so a quite young woman, but not a child bride. The ideal age for a team of oxen is also perhaps a bit greater than we might expect: nine-year-olds are good workers and won't struggle against each other in the furrow (436).

Boeotia: Rustic Backwater or Cultural Crossroads?

Even in English, 'Boeotian' is a byword for obtuse philistinism, for country-bumpkin backwardness. Fifth-century Athenian playwrights enjoyed mocking their neighbours with the stereotype of dim-witted rube. The poet Pindar, despite being Boeotian himself, uses the slur 'Boeotian sow' in his sixth Olympian Ode: it isn't clear who is being insulted, or why, but the hayseed gist of the jeer seems straightforward enough. No doubt Hesiod's own description of his hometown of Askra as 'Bad in winter, harsh in summer, not/ Ever pleasant' (640) contributes to the perception of a hillbilly Boeotia. At first glance, Boeotia hardly seems ideal for producing one of the first poets in Western literature, not to mention arguably the original economist and philosopher, whose work is also one of the earliest texts, very possibly the first of any length, set down in the Greek alphabet.

But how much of a backwater can Boeotia be if some of the very earliest Greek poetry (Hesiod) and some of its most difficult and lofty lyrics (Pindar) come out of it? Herodotus, writing his history in the fifth century BCE, related that the alphabet itself was introduced into Greece, specifically at Boeotia, by Cadmus, in legend a Phoenician prince and the traditional founder of Thebes. Thebes, Boeotia's principal city, was in turn an exporter of mythology, from Cadmus and the dragon's teeth to Oedipus and the Sphinx to the Seven Against Thebes to Hercules. The god Dionysus, though the son of Zeus, is also, on the distaff side, Cadmus' grandson, and would have been conceived (if that is the right word for a blast of lightning) in Boeotia. As Byron points out in his notes to *Childe Harold's Pilgrimage*, Boeotia was where the first riddle was posed – the Sphinx's description of man as four-legged in the morning, two-legged at noon and three-legged at the close of day. Hesiod seems to nod to this tale with his three-legged old man; i.e., man hobbling on a cane (533).

It's worth wondering why Hesiod's father might have chosen to settle in Boeotia in the first place. There was evidently an ancient kinship between the Boeotians and the Aeolians, but perhaps Boeotia also offered opportunity as well as hardship, available homesteads, say, of arable land. (Pausanias in the second century CE describes Mount Helikon as 'one of the mountains of Greece with the most fertile soil and the greatest number of cultivated trees'.)[6] As an economic migrant from Asia Minor, Hesiod's father is fleeing 'Not wealth nor riches nor prosperity,/ But Evil Need' (637–8), seeking a better life. While Hesiod is hardly sentimental about Askra, he feels sufficiently bound to his (presumably) native place that he establishes a cult to the Muses there, and immortalizes the town in verse. His grumblings about Askra have something of a local curmudgeon's contrarian boast about them.

If we doubt the prestige and centrality, geographically and imaginatively, of Boeotia for Greece in antiquity, a simple corrective is to glance at the Catalogue of Ships in Book 2 of the *Iliad* (*Il.* 2.494ff.), that joint celebration of Panhellenic pride and local patriotism. It begins with Boeotia, the region grandly heading the whole armada of place names with fifty ships, each manned by 120 young rowers – a force 6,000 strong.

Boeotia also lies alongside one of the only places in the Greek world which, rather than stagnating in population and contracting in cultural outlook during the 'Dark Ages', throve and expanded its interactions with places and peoples far beyond it shores, the long fertile island of Euboea (the 'Rich in Cattle'). Euboea is the Dark Age's bright spot. Second in size only to Crete among the Greek isles, it is separated from Boeotia by, at the narrowest point of the Euripus Strait, a mere 125 feet. The archaeological site at Lefkandi, between Chalcis and Eretria, on the shore facing the mainland, opposite Aulis, reveals a prosperous, outward-looking society, trading and interacting with distant ports of call, in a revival that lasted until the mid-ninth century BCE. (A grand burial there from 1000 BCE eerily evokes some details from Patroclus' funeral in the *Iliad*, including the sacrifice of four horses, cremated remains in a brazen urn, as well as a female skeleton wearing a golden brassiere, and sporting a Babylonian bauble itself a millennium old at the time of interment, with an iron knife suggestive of sacrifice nuzzled at her throat.) Euboean seafarers zipped across the Mediterranean, forming a 'hotline' between Greeks and cultures to the east and west.[7] Euboean pottery abounds at sites as far east as al-Mina, in northern Syria, and Euboean cities founded numerous settlements and trading posts, including to the west in Italy.

If Hesiod has answered a regional call for poets to participate in the funeral games at Chalcis, Askra isn't so far off the beaten path after all: it's directly connected to one of the most important metropolises (literally 'mother cities') of the archaic Greek world. Despite the difficulties and dangers of travel – broken axles on overladen wagons and the watery grave of shipwreck are two mentioned in *Works and Days* – Hesiod's is not a static, stay-at-home sort of world, but one of opening horizons, widespread trade, far-flung Greek outposts with freedom of movement, cultural festivals that drew participants from the greater region, and the social mobility implicit in Hesiod's father's striking out westward to find a finer way of life. 'With boats, admire the small,/ But load a large one' (643) is not quite as homespun a proverb as our own 'don't put all your eggs in one basket': it's the aphorism of travellers and traders.

Boeotia, it turns out, was not a bad place to be born a poet in the mid- to late eighth century BCE, especially if you happened to have colonial parents and to have made a personal visit to the nearby cultural crossroads of the island of Euboea.

'Are You Suggesting Hesiod Was Really in a Legal Wrangle with His Brother?'

Do I think Hesiod was a real person? I had never considered otherwise until stopped short by an incredulous question during an informal presentation. Did I *really* think Hesiod had a brother Perses with whom he was embroiled in a lawsuit? My immediate response was: who would make up being from *Askra*? Or why confess your sole 'sea-journey' was a bay-crossing jaunt of a couple of kilometres from Aulis to Chalcis, unless to savour the real irony of it, being the son of an old salt? Still, I had to think harder about why I took Hesiod at his word.

Certainly, we will read *Works and Days* differently if we take the theoretical tack that Hesiod is less a person than a rubric under which certain kinds of topics or proverbs were compiled. As a writer and translator myself, as a practitioner, I am much more sympathetic to the idea that even anonymous works are composed by someone, even bad lines are committed by somebody, and good and great poems more so. (I don't deny that there are a very few great literary works authored by committee, the King James Bible arguably being one, and yet, even that committee had particular members, and for that matter they were revising Tyndale's masterpiece.) Anonymous might be better termed 'unattributed'.

Not everyone, however, is of the opinion that Hesiod was a real person, or that, if he was, he had a brother named Perses, or if he did, that they scraped by in a dismal hamlet called Askra.[8] Perhaps that I live in Greece where nearly everyone *is* in fact in a lawsuit with his brother over their patrimony, and quite a lot of people descend from Asia Minor émigrés who have fallen on hard times, and everyone complains about corruption and the courts, adds to my bias that Hesiod is based in fact. But I would also add that, for me, besides making *Works and Days* more compelling, many complicated Hesiodic problems are clarified by taking statements as essentially true or roughly factual, whereas making them sophisticated fictions stirs up more murky problems than it answers.

That Hesiod's father, an unsuccessful sea merchant, moves in the counterintuitive direction, from Aeolian Kyme (that is, on the coast of modern Turkey just south of Lesbos) to mainland Greece has the sad, sour smack of actual failure: ninth- and eighth-century migration tended on the whole to be towards settlements and outposts. (Interestingly, the places where the Aeolic dialect appear in *Works and Days* are precisely those concerning Hesiod's father or the sea – as if he hears his father's accent.) Coincidentally, or maybe not, Aeolian Kyme was synonymous at a later period in the ancient world with poor financial judgement and debt. For 300 years, it is said, they failed to realize that as a port city they could make money from harbour taxes.

I like to think that Hesiod's father set out first for the trading island of Euboea, crossed the strait and went as far inland as he could go without once more catching sight of the treacherous sea. Thus he would have ended up on the eastern side of Mount Helikon, which, had he climbed it, would have offered a view of the Corinthian Gulf. Instead, it was dry land as far as the eye could reach, even if it did mean settling in a village cut off from cooling sea breezes in summer and subject to extremes of cold in the winter.

Hesiod's father might have potentially interacted not only with fellow Greeks, but with other ethnicities and languages as well. Perhaps his father's trading background helps explain Hesiod's familiarity with Near Eastern thought and mythology. Some of his father's own sailors might have been Phoenician; maybe some could write a bit.

As for the question of Perses – flesh-and-blood brother or literary device – one of the main arguments for the latter seems to be his name. That it means something like 'wastrel', the argument goes, makes it implausibly convenient. But the very oddness of the name could also be a point for its authenticity. Perses, that great blockhead, shares his name with a Titan in Hesiod's *Theogony*, who happens to be 'pre-eminent of them all in wisdom' (*Th.* 377). This Perses is the father of the goddess Hekate, who is, according to the *Theogony*, perhaps the greatest deity besides Zeus himself. Hekate had a popular cult in Caria (Asia Minor). If Hesiod's family were adherents to this cult, naming a son after an associated deity seems in keeping.

Although the tradition of wisdom literature is already ancient in the East when Hesiod is composing, there, as in more recent wisdom literature in Western literature, the addressee tends to be either a ruler or prince or a son (consider Machiavelli's *The Prince* or, in *Hamlet*, Polonius' paternal advice 'neither a borrower nor a lender be'). The innovation of addressing a brother might emerge rather naturally from exasperation with an actual sibling, a common enough human condition.

Scholars and theorists might tend to argue one way about this, and poets and verse translators another, claiming authority, Hesiod-fashion, directly from the Muses.

An excess of caution regarding the ultimately unknowable diminishes the pleasure, it seems to me, of reading this work as a direct communication across the millennia. As Samuel Butler says in his delightfully quirky yet insightful work on Homer, *The Authoress of the Odyssey*, 'Men of science, so far as I have observed them, are apt in their fear of jumping to a conclusion to forget that there is such a thing as jumping away from one.'[9]

End of the So-Called Dark Ages and Dawn of a New Technology

In the eighth century, Greece was emerging from a time of cultural eclipse traditionally known as the Greek Dark Ages, the era between the thirteenth and ninth centuries BCE, during which writing mysteriously vanishes. The Mycenaean palaces had used a syllabary form of writing, 'Linear-B'. Linear-B disappears, almost overnight, with the collapse of the palatial system and its attendant red tape.

Then, after centuries in Greece with no writing at all, suddenly, in the mid-eighth century, inscriptions in an entirely different method of writing Greek appear. The onset and spread of this new system is likewise swift, from no evidence of it in the ninth century to scribbles in the last third of the eighth century that seem to indicate that regular people, not professional scribes, are sufficiently comfortable with it to scratch out jokes from drinking games. Potters, arguably not the most sophisticated element of society, are early adepts. Borrowing a score of symbols from the consonantal Western Semitic script used by the seafaring Phoenicians, adding some Greek-specific letters to the end of the alphabet (Phi, Chi, and Psi for instance) and repurposing other symbols to make vowels, the Greek alphabet seems to appear rather suddenly and almost fully formed.

'So and so made me.' 'This is mine.' 'I belong to so and so.' 'I [object speaking] am dedicated to the god.' The earliest alphabetic inscriptions are public pronouncements, by private individuals or on behalf of individuals, of a kind still familiar to us. One of the very oldest inscription we have (*c.*740 BCE), on the famous Dipylon Wine Jug, found in the Kerameikos cemetery of Athens, literally the 'potters field', has scratched upon it, right to left, Semitic fashion, in hexameter, 'Whoever of all the dancers now dances most nimbly, to him . . .' before trailing off into some other letters in another hand. It is a trophy for a contest, one that included dancing and therefore music and, we might well assume, poetry as well. Another of the oldest inscriptions in the Greek (indeed, the Euboean) alphabet comes from the island of Ischia, in modern Italy – three lines of playful dactylic hexameter, scratched out right to left on a clay wine cup – along the lines of '[I am] Nestor's cup, good to drink from / whosoever drinks from this, desire will seize him / for beautifully crowned Aphrodite.'

Thus one of the curiosities of the reintroduction to Greece of writing is that, whereas Linear-B seems to have been used, at least in the clay tablets that have come down to us, principally for palatial administration, lists and tax receipts, the very earliest Greek alphabetic inscriptions are simple personal assertions of possession and/or lines of verse, almost all in the metre of Homer and of Hesiod, namely, dactylic hexameter.

The great and deceptively simple innovation of the Greek alphabet was the addition of vowels, in which the spoken language abounds. (Consider Keats's description of Greek's 'vowel'd undersong' in his poem 'Lamia'.) Quite a few Greek words are entirely made up of vowels, such as Aeaea, Circe's island, and thus impossible to write without them. Hesiod's own name – 'Hesiodos' in transliterated Greek – reduced to consonants alone, would be SDS, nearly undecipherable. On the other hand, with the complex syllabary script of the Mycenaeans, Linear-B, you still had to guess at the vowels or even the number of syllables in a word. If, for instance, our three-syllable word 'elephant' were written in a syllabary, it might come out something like La-Pa-Na-Ta, intelligible by context maybe but not by sounding it out, and unscannable in a metrical poem requiring three syllables in that position, not four.

So while there were previous scripts that relied on readers' conjectures based on sound clues, the Greek alphabet, by adding vowels – which appears to have been a singular, critical event, and thus conceivably the innovation of one individual[10] – is arguably the first system that allowed for something approaching sound recording, a musical notation of the human voice. The alphabet, with its precise articulation of words into syllables, turned out to be ideal for the recording of metrical poetry.

Is it possible that the alphabet was even invented for the notation of poetry, and found other purposes later?[11] Aside from potters branding their wares, the early alphabet does not appear to be used for any more widespread commercial purpose. Numbers in alphabetical inscriptions discovered thus far do not appear for another 200 years.

However it was, the composition of Hesiod's poems roughly coincided with the period of the reintroduction of writing into Greece, and his autobiographical verses were no doubt scratched out quite early on in the alphabet's own life story. Pausanias, writing in the second century CE, claimed to have been shown by native Askrans the original leaden sheet on which *Works and Days* was inscribed. While this leaden sheet might not have been a 'manuscript' in Hesiod's hand, I think it likely Pausanias did indeed view something already very old by his time, something, as it were, authentic.

The evidence points to Euboea as the vector whereby the Greek alphabet 'went viral': it is the Euboean script that arrives in the colony of Tyrrhenian Cumae (in modern Italy), and, adjusted for the Etruscan language, becomes the Latin alphabet forming the very words you are reading now. If Hesiod did indeed perform a poem on Euboea, might he have found there someone who was able to jot it down? Perhaps he even mastered the newfangled method himself for his second poem, the much more personal and discursive *Works and Days*.

Curiously, modern Greece presents precisely such an example of a talented but illiterate wordsmith who learns to read and write as an adult, the Greek War of Independence general Yannis Makriyannis (1797–1864). The twentieth-century poet and Nobel Laureate George Seferis declared Makriyannis one of the two greatest Greek prose stylists. Makriyannis was unlettered, but taught himself the painstaking act of writing in order to compose his *Memoirs*, a first-hand account of the Greek War of Independence. Innocent of book learning, he composed it in a pure demotic Greek, with vernacular verve. Why couldn't Hesiod too have learned to write in order to compose or record his poems?[12]

Potters are among the first to use the alphabet, branding

their wares; poets would not have been far behind. (Hesiod, remember, lumps potters and poets together.) An oral bard doesn't need to slap his name or his life story on his poem – he authors it by uttering it. But one of the advantages of writing a poem down is that you can put your name or your 'bio' in the verses – you can sign it, if you will. And your words are still yours even when you aren't voicing them. The early alphabet likes to declare ownership or belonging, and it speaks in the first person.

Who Came First? Homer or Hesiod

'As to the age of Hesiod and Homer, I have conducted very careful researches into this matter, but I do not like to write on the subject, as I know the quarrelsome nature of those especially who constitute the modern school of epic criticism.' – Pausanias[13]

Recent readers and scholars have tended to assume Homer is earlier than Hesiod (I certainly started this project with that assumption), but there isn't conclusive evidence for this. Largely it is a general perception given by their respective subject matter: Homer is writing about an already antique Bronze Age glorious past as opposed to Hesiod's problematic Iron Age present in *Works and Days*.[14]

In general, for the ancients, Homer and Hesiod were more or less contemporaries (Herodotus claimed they were, and placed them, at most, four centuries older than himself), with, if anything, Hesiod as the elder. A text by the fourth-century BCE sophist Alcidamas fictionally pits Homer and Hesiod in a singing contest, set, of course, on Euboea; Homer is portrayed as the younger contemporary. In lists of the first poets from the dawn of time, the traditional ordering, suggesting chronology, has Orpheus, Musaeus, Hesiod and Homer, with Orpheus and Musaeus considered legendary. The intriguing if mysterious Parian Marble inscription (third century BCE) puts the 'appearance' of Hesiod some thirty years before Homer, a space of a generation or two. The nineteenth- and early twentieth-century German scholars Ulrich von Wilamowitz-Moellendorff and Erich Bethe both assumed Hesiod had priority, as did Hesiod's great editor and commenter Martin West, many of whose ideas infuse this essay. I have come around to this opinion, 'gradually, then suddenly'. The evidence suggests, at any rate, that Hesiod's poems were set down in writing before the *Iliad* and *Odyssey*, at least in the form that the Homeric epics have come down to us.

There are some moments or passages in Hesiod and Homer that seem to suggest some kind of direct connection (as opposed to both emerging from the mulch of the same tradition and conventions). While it isn't obvious in which direction the influence flows, for me, the Hesiod to Homer direction solves problems that the opposite introduces.

Hesiod is certainly aware of the story of Troy, the war over Helen, which he views from the local perspective of a naval expedition setting out from Boeotia. Hesiod might have known some of the same passages that the Catalogue of Ships (*Il.* 2.494ff.) draws on in its mustering of the armada against Troy. Hesiod wears his considerable and sometimes arcane learning lightly in *Works and Days*, that is part of its (and his) charm, but he would seem either to have no knowledge of the *Iliad* itself, or, less likely to my view, to eschew any specific reference to it. It isn't that Hesiod is unwilling to make an allusion. *Works and Days* is aware of itself as a sort of sequel to the *Theogony* (just as the *Odyssey* is very aware of the *Iliad*), constantly making adjustments and elaborations to the assertions and tales of the earlier poem.

The *Iliad* doesn't seem to be aware of Hesiod either, with one niggling exception: the mention of the 'son' of an 'Amphidamas' in the *Iliad* (*Il.* 23.87). It is the sons of great-hearted Amphidamas, we remember, who have arranged the funeral games at which Hesiod wins the poetry competition and his tripod. By itself, the mention of the name could be mere coincidence, but coming as it does in a book about a funeral games where tripods are awarded as prizes makes for a couple of points of connection.

And surely Hesiod brags about an actual prize that he is keen to name and date, rather than making something up with an obscure reference to Homer. It makes much more sense to me that the composer of the *Iliad*, or some later editor, needing a name of a certain metrical length to insert into the backstory of Patroclus (who appears to Achilles as a ghost), in the direct run-up to his funeral games, should elegantly hit upon Hesiod's Amphidamas, associated with just such a games.

While the matter is not settled, I do hope that readers will at least consider that there is no automatic reason that Homer should confidently be considered the more ancient author besides hunch and habit (I argue as a poet translator), and there are on the contrary some good reasons to be suspicious of this. The possibility that Hesiod is a contemporary or older changes our perception of him and his poems.

A Modern Bard?

Might the audience have experienced something in Hesiod exciting and new? Not a performer improvising a familiar battle scene with the aid of formulae and convention, but someone reciting a fixed 'text' *from memory*, compositions very different from traditional epic and, furthermore, radically different from one another. The *Theogony* unfolds the origins of the cosmos ('in the beginning was Chaos') as well as the family trees of the gods, while in *Works and Days* the poet refreshingly takes his own trials and tribulations for a subject, and depicts the workaday world as his audience knew it, as well as the history not of the gods, but of humanity itself from its creation to the current Iron Age.

A comparison with the performers depicted in the Homeric epics suggests how innovative Hesiod may potentially be. There are no bards as such in the action of the *Iliad*. The only character to sing is Achilles himself, who does so to delight his own heart, and he has no audience besides his companion Patroclus (*Il.* 9.190ff.). His subject is the traditional one for a minstrel, though; accompanying himself on a phorminx – a kind of lyre – Achilles sings of the 'glorious deeds of men', or as Fagles' translation has it, 'the famous deeds of fighting heroes'.[15] This is the fit theme for a singer.

In contrast, in the *Odyssey*, bards are everywhere, regaling noblemen at banquets with the deeds of heroes or even the adventures of the gods. On the human plane, the poem practically opens with a sweep across the lyre's strings, as the bard Phemius warms up the entertainment for yet another banquet of the suitors (his theme: the return of heroes from Troy, a sore topic). The fame and glory these singers trade in is the celebrity of their subjects, not their own. Admittedly, the bard Demodocus in *Odyssey*, Book 8 is a star in his own right, portrayed with such affection that he becomes the basis for our image of

Homer, revered and blind. But Odysseus sings the bard's
praises precisely because Demodocus sings his. (Odysseus
has a request: 'Odysseus and the Trojan Horse'.) Demo-
docus is noble, Phemius, the bard at Ithaka, is craven:
during the slaughter of the suitors he begs for his life, after
carefully setting down his instrument, perhaps the first
case of 'don't shoot the piano player'. But both bards are
'divine singers', inspired professionals. 'The lyre is the
companion of the rich feast' (Od. 8.99). This is the
Homeric picture of traditional poets and performers.

Hesiod, like the composer or composers of the Homeric
epics, comes at the end of a long line of traditional, skilled,
improvising, professional oral performers. (I say 'end',
though I don't mean to imply that such bards suddenly
ceased to perform or matter.) Though he is clearly steeped
in the dialect and metrical conventions of epic poetry,
Hesiod presents himself as an amateur, shepherd- or
farmer-cum-minstrel, suddenly inspired by the Muses
with a poetic gift, deciding to take his chances at a
regional festival. He was rewarded for his pains with a
Major Prize, which I would say again suggests he had in
some way set himself apart in performance, composition
or both. It seems clear that innovation could be esteemed
and even perhaps driven by the prevalent poetic contest
culture in Greece in later centuries. As Telemachus says in
the Odyssey: 'Men praise the song the most that comes
freshest to their ears' (Od. 1.351–2). After all, what is a
poetry contest but Hesiod's 'Good Strife', the spirit of
competition that leads envious poets to try to outdo each
other in ambition and originality?

Hesiod is at pains to mark the poems as belonging to
him, to claim authorship. He speaks of his poetic epiph-
any and gives his name in the Theogony, and stamps

Works and Days with an idiosyncratic autobiography, a set of circumstances which would be as awkward for another bard to lay claim to as implausible to have any motive for so doing. It is by the written word that the ephemeral authorship and glory of the oral bard is transformed into something that carries over and beyond the occasion of the song's utterance: Hesiod's insertion of himself into his songs is at the very least an indication, as West remarks, that the poems were written down at no great distance in time from their composition. West observes too that the relative brevity of Hesiod's poems – *Works and Days* as we have it is a scant 828 lines, to the *Iliad*'s whopping 15,693 – and occasional creakiness of their construction might also be symptomatic of someone's wrestling with a new medium.

Sceptre and Tripod: Symbols of Authority

The standard attribute for a Homeric bard is the lyre, the marker of his status and profession. Hesiod seems not to have played one; he speaks of lyrists as separate from singers (*Th.* 95), and an apocryphal story related by Pausanias says that Hesiod was expelled from a competition in Delphi because he hadn't learned how to accompany himself. It is striking in the *Theogony*, that the Muses who make a poet out of Hesiod present him not with a musical instrument but a stick.[16] The laurel staff is a symbol not of singing, but of authority to speak at an assembly, as Odysseus' sceptre in the *Iliad* (2.186).

The sceptre, obtained in a supernatural encounter with the daughters of Zeus (the Muses), is of course eminently appropriate for the subject matter of the *Theogony*, the origins of the cosmos and the genealogy of the gods. It would have made an impressive prop too ('I have this staff directly from the Muses!'), and would have given Hesiod the authority to speak on the sublime, and in the presence of royalty.

In *Works and Days*, however, Hesiod presents himself in a humbler light. Though he begins by invoking the Muses, in the down-to-earth world of the poem, poets are not so much divinely inspired as competitive members of a skilled trade or guild, and perhaps not an entirely reputable one – they are mentioned in the same breath as beggars. Here, Hesiod's authority as a poet comes from winning a competition, judged by mortals. That his authority is as an official Prize-Winning Poet perfectly suits the poem's themes of judgements and justice. The tangible symbol of this victory is the weight and status of the bronze tripod, which, if we go by the poem, was on display in Helikon for anyone to take a gander at it. Pausanias, writing in the second century CE, would claim to have been shown Hesiod's actual tripod at Askra.

An ingenious and relatively recent suggestion[17] claims that the hymn which won Hesiod the contest on Euboea was in fact his earlier *Theogony*. With its passage on poetry's power to assuage a recent grief, and its compliment to kings (here definitely *not* eaters of bribes), the *Theogony* seems perfectly pitched to win over Amphidamas' bereaved sons. Likewise, in its curious panegyric to the goddess Hekate we find the list of those she assists indifferently suited to Boeotian Askra, but spot on for an Euboean audience. She is an ally of horsemen (Chalcis supported a cavalry), athletes, such as might compete at a funeral games, and fishermen, who would have been scarce on the ground in the piedmont of Askra, but plentiful enough at Chalcis on the coast.

Perhaps Hesiod's mention of it seems to us off-hand, but a tripod is nothing to sneeze at. In the *Iliad*, for instance, in Book 22.164, we are informed that the appropriate prize for the horse or prestigious chariot race at a funeral games was a bronze tripod or a woman. In the actual funeral games for Patroclus, first prize is a tripod and a woman (cf. *Il.* 23.262–5). In the wrestling match in those games, first prize was a tripod 'worth twelve oxen', second prize, a woman 'worth four oxen' (Il. 23.702–5). Keep in mind that in the world of *Works and Days*, owning even a single ox is of material advantage. A bronze tripod might be worth, in other words, a small fortune, and Hesiod dedicates his to the Muses in a local sanctuary, at a time when tripods in Boeotia are dedicated at only a couple of sites of Panhellenic importance.

Muses, First and Last

That Hesiod brings the tripod home should perhaps give us pause. At least in later times these grand prizes, potentially heavy, not easily portable like a wreath, were usually inscribed and left *in situ* to advertise the glory of the victor and his community. Herodotus, writing over two centuries years later, describes an occurrence from the festival of Triopian Apollo, where the judges awarded tripods to the winners; victors were not to carry them away from the holy place, but to dedicate them to the god. A man from Herodotus' native Halicarnassus who hauled his home incurred a punishment on his hometown, which was barred afterwards from participating in the games.

If Hesiod does indeed trundle home to Askra with a tripod and dedicate it to the Muses in their eponymous valley, this may well have been a 'revolutionary gesture'[18]

on his part, in the process establishing their cult. Perhaps
there had been a local spot dedicated to some mountain
nymphs known as the Muses (a cult evidently brought out
of Thrace). Muses traditionally reside on mountains; one
etymology of 'muse' connects them with towering places.[19]
Hesiod, however, connects the etymology of the name
'Muse' in Greek to memory and mind. The first to declare
that the Muses are the daughters of Mnemosyne, 'Mem-
ory', he is also the first to spell out their nine names – the
Lovely Voiced, the Many Hymned, the Delighter in Dance,
the Giver of Fame, and so on. Hesiod describes, in the
Theogony, a direct interaction, a religious conversion, in
which he is changed from shepherd to divinely inaugu-
rated bard. Wade-Gery points out the striking similarities
to the nativity story in the Gospel of St Luke.[20] Hesiod,
pasturing his flock by night – the star-gazing poet
describes the Muses as 'night-striders' (*Th.* 10) – comes
upon divine singing beings who teach him to celebrate the
birth of God, or the gods.

I do not doubt that Hesiod did experience some epiphanic
moment in the mountains. Poets of much more recent vin-
tage have based their authority on a divine or supernatural
experience: Wordsworth communing with sublime Nature
in the *Prelude*, Yeats, with his automatic writing, Angelos
Sikelianos, who thought he could raise the dead, or James
Merrill communing with the spirits on his Ouiji board.
The first recorded English poem we have was by a North-
umbrian poet named Caedmon of the seventh century CE,
a cowherd, who, according to the Venerable Bede, was
approached at night by an angel and bidden to sing of
things since the beginning of creation. In a further strange
resemblance to Hesiod, Caedmon could not play the harp,
the standard accoutrement for an Old English bard.

In the *Iliad*, the Muse operates as a connection with tradition, a device to move the story or segue from one action to another, or a conduit to knowledge of events clouded by the passage of time. In Hesiod, the Muses are both literary and literal, reigning, importantly, over both truth and outright fiction. The Muses, as we remember, present Hesiod with, not a musical instrument, but an abstract symbol of authority, the sceptre. As Charles Segal says, 'Hesiod thus detaches the empowering sign of poetic craft from the act of singing and from the immediate performative context. In this respect he is operating in a zone of greater speculative freedom about his art than did Homer.'[21] If Hesiod's poems were composed and even written down before being recited, the etymological connection Hesiod makes between Muse and Mind, and Muse and Memory, becomes even more significant. The dedication of his victory tripod in honour of the Muses also establishes Hesiod's poetic authority beyond the ephemeral moment of performance. Homeric bards preserve the glory of others in their song; Hesiod establishes the posterity of poets themselves.

It has been suggested that the Muses are unique to Greece, that they are the most Hellenic of goddesses. Nearly all other Greek deities correspond to figures in Middle Eastern and/or Indo-European mythologies. The Muses, though, whether of Olympus or Helikon, are both stubbornly local and Panhellenic. In Hesiod's narrative of becoming a poet, the Muses grant him the gift of song; he in turn dedicates a tripod to them, enshrining his victory in their valley, Helikon, his backyard. They discover him, as it were; but it is arguable that Hesiod also invents the Muses, certainly as we think of them, complete with their names and number, their entwined DNA of memory and forgetfulness, fact and fantasy, their personality of fickle wilfulness and wily wisdom. Herodotus says that it is Homer and Hesiod who first ascribe to the gods their various attributes. It is intriguing to consider that Hesiod, the first poet personality in Western literature, might also have been the one to introduce the goddesses of inspiration to the Western imagination.

Themes and Structure of the Poem
Sibling Rivalry

Works and Days is roiled with anxiety about conflict between siblings. In the first assertion of the poem, Hesiod announces that Strife herself is a sister; rivalry is a sibling. In the *Theogony*, Strife was an only child; here she is a twin. The first-born Strife is the good Strife, the spirit of competition that drives innovation and ambition; the younger bad Strife is destructive conflict. (Pausanias says that the leaden sheet of *Works and Days* he was shown by the Askrans started not with the preamble we have now, but jumped right in with the line about 'There are, not one, but *two* Strifes' (11–12).)

Hard on the heels of the two Strifes, Hesiod introduces the story of Pandora and the jar into Western literature. In Hesiod's elaboration of the story in *Works and Days*, Epimetheus is warned by his clever brother not to accept a gift from Zeus. It is worth noting that by ignoring his wise brother's advice (Perses, listen up!), Epimetheus is partly responsible for the jar of troubles unleashed on mankind.

The tale of the jar is followed by the Five Ages of Man, which charts a progression (or decadence rather) of metals from Gold to Iron, possibly an Eastern trope that

Hesiod Hellenizes by interrupting the metallic progression with the utterly Greek 'Age of Heroes'. We expect the expedition to Troy in the Age of Heroes. The story of Seven Against Thebes would have had clear Boeotian relevance, but it is perhaps also included for its theme of strife among siblings: the war over Oedipus' property is a war between his sons over their inheritance.

Hesiod prophesies that the end of our own race (the Iron one) on the earth will be marked by a number of evils; the end of brotherly love is one. Family prosperity, furthermore, can only really be guaranteed by a single son; two or more risk conflict. It is worth considering that even the funeral games at which Hesiod performs have fraternal associations: it is won at an event established by Amphidamas' sons, that is to say, a set of brothers honouring their father's legacy in noble splendour, as opposed to petty legal squabbling.

All this contributes to my impression that the purported dispute with Perses was an actual one, not merely a framing device for the wisdom genre.

Wider Justice

Sometimes the poem is addressed not to Perses, but to the presiding judges. It is at them that the allegory of the nightingale and the hawk is ostensibly aimed. A hawk clutches a nightingale in his talons; when she protests, he tells her she should submit to his greater force, that to struggle 'adds suffering to shame' (211). The word for nightingale in Greek means 'singer', and so it is hard not to associate the poet with the pitiable songster, even though the hawk seems to come out ahead.

At first, we aren't sure how to take this; the fable seems to run counter to Hesiod's concern with fairness. But maybe the fable's placement provides a key: it is inserted after that woeful view of the world, the Five Ages of Man, which peters out into a potential near future where god-fearing decency has deserted humanity; and right before Perses himself is warned against arrogance and urged to strive for justice.

Hesiod seems to leave the fable up in the air (as it were), but later clarifies the moral for Perses and the judges alike. Even in this fallen world, broken oaths and corrupt judgements do not go unremarked; it is Zeus himself who, with his many invisible supernatural spies, sees all. Cities prosper based on their observance of justice (for citizen and foreigner alike – the natural concern perhaps of the son of an immigrant), while the wickedness of a single man can bring down famine, pestilence and war. (In myth, both Oedipus and Agamemnon bring plagues upon their people by misdeeds.)

Then, elegantly, Hesiod comes back around to the allegory of animals, turning again to Perses (274–80):

> So Perses, mull these matters in your mind,
> Give ear to Justice; leave Force far behind.
> For Kronos' son gave justice to mankind,
> The fish and beasts and winged birds of the air
> Eat one another – they don't have a share
> Of law and right – he made the law for man,
> And this way is by far the better plan.

In the animal kingdom might makes right. Not so for mankind: men have law. The animal allegory is suddenly no allegory at all, precisely because it is about animals.

The Gospel of Work

After this disquisition on justice, Hesiod drops the judges or kings altogether from the poem; the focus is on Perses, who himself gradually fades into the background. Justice involves a right relationship with Zeus, the king of the gods and giver of moral law. But this right relation to the world does not only involve giving honest judgements; man can only be kept on a right footing by work. In another refinement to the *Theogony*'s Prometheus story, in *Works and Days* Zeus not only takes fire away from mankind for Prometheus' trickery, but also hides the means of living; originally, food produced itself. Prometheus steals fire, but cannot return mankind to a time before work.

In Hesiod's view, the human and the divine are out of kilter. Work is the punishment for Prometheus' original sin, but also the redemption. Working and good management forestall famine and bring prosperity. A little foresight – having ready the boards you need to make a wagon, keeping an eye out for timber for the plough – and planting and harvest done in the right way at the right season may put you in the enviable position of being able to give rather than receive. Poverty is not shameful in and of itself – it too is Zeus-given – but laziness and shiftlessness bring on the scorn of your neighbours and their reluctance to come to your aid. Work 'Endears you to the immortals' (309).

Hesiod concludes the poem with his almanac of lucky and unlucky days: there is a right and a wrong time for any given activity, whether it be setting up a loom or gelding a calf, opening a jar (perhaps Pandora broached her jar on an unlucky day) or begetting a child.

Hesiod marks time in at least three ways in the almanac and hemerology section of *Works and Days*. There are lunar months (whose names varied in Greece by region), each divided into waxing and waning halves. The days of the month were also numbered, and there is a division somewhat akin to a week (that most arbitrary of the units of time), so that you can refer to the second fifth of the month, for instance. (In modern Greek, too, most of the days of the week are referred to by ordinal numbers: the second, Deutera, is Monday, the third, Triti, is Tuesday, and so on.) There are the risings and settings of certain constellations, a sidereal calendar. And there is phenology – when the first cuckoo calls, for instance, or when cranes cry in the sky in their migrations, or when the yellow thistle blows and the cicada chirrs, when the topmost leaf on the fig tree is the size of a crow's foot.

Despite the pessimism, or rather pejorism, of the Five Ages of Man, Hesiod concludes the poem (or such is the ending we have) with a reassuring vision of a universe governed by reason and justice, by rules and ritual, in which a wise and hard-working man may prosper. The man who knows the lore of days, who avoids overstepping the bounds of law and decency, and who in his work is blameless in the eyes of the gods, is happy and rich: or, in the phrase made popular in Benjamin Franklin's *Poor Richard's Almanac*, 'healthy, wealthy, and wise'. It's the gospel of work, whereby honest toil can better one's lot and put one on a right footing with the human and the divine and the life-giving earth, even in a dark, an Iron, a belated age.

NOTES

1. *Greek Dark Ages*: Modern scholars find this term has too negative a connotation. 'Iron Age' also covers this era, but has a specific meaning for Hesiod, so I will hew to 'Dark Ages' for the period when writing vanishes from Greece.
2. *the Greek alphabet*: Although there were initially an assortment of regional variations, so that it is more correct to say 'alphabets', I will use the singular as a shorthand to indicate the technology as a whole.
3. Line numbers throughout for *Works and Days* refer to the Greek original, and are thus only approximate as regards the English translation.
4. As in the Book of Judges, where the judges are unelected chieftains or leaders as well as arbiters of disputes.
5. *fourteen or fifteen, maybe later*: Aristotle, writing in the fourth century BCE, gives fourteen as the average age. Diet and nutrition are factors.
6. *'one of the mountains ... cultivated trees'*: Pausanias, *Description of Greece*, vol. 4, trans. W. H. S. Jones Loeb Classical Library (Cambridge, Mass.: Harvard University Press, 1935).
7. *Euboean seafarers ... east and west*: See Robin Lane Fox, *Travelling Heroes: Greeks and Their Myths in the Epic Age of Homer* (London: Allen Lane, 2008).
8. *Not everyone ... Askra*: For the view that the name Hesiod represents a type of Panhellenic poetry gathered under this name rather than an actual individual, see particularly Gregory Nagy, 'Hesiod and the Ancient Biographical Traditions', in *Brill's Companion to Hesiod*, ed. F. Montanari, A. Rengakos and C. Tsagalis (Leiden: Brill, 2009), pp. 271–311. For a more layman-friendly version of the same view, see Robert Lamberton, 'Introduction', in *Works and Days and Theogony*, trans. Stanley Lombardo (Indianapolis/Cambridge, Mass.: Hackett Publishing, 1993).

9. *'Men of science ... away from one'*: Samuel Butler, *The Authoress of the Odyssey* (London: Longmans, Green and Co., 1897), p. 189.

10. *the innovation of one individual*: See Barry B. Powell, *Homer and the Origin of the Greek Alphabet* (Cambridge: Cambridge University Press, 1991). He suggests it may even have been Homer himself who made this innovation. I don't quite buy this, and anyway place Hesiod before Homer, but it is an extremely attractive idea that an individual, maybe even a Phoenician, perhaps named Cadmus, who found himself in Greece, tweaked the script to the new language. At any rate, the innovation requires an overlap of Phoenicians and Greeks.

11. *the alphabet was even invented ... later*: Again, as far as I can tell, the suggestion that the alphabet was invented for the purpose of recording poetry first occurs in H. T. Wade-Gery's 1949 lecture on Hesiod and Homer, 'The Poet's Circumstances', in *The Poet of the Iliad* (Cambridge: Cambridge University Press, 1952).

12. *Why couldn't Hesiod too ... record his poems?*: Powell suggests exactly this of Homer (*Homer and the Origin of the Greek Alphabet*): that he learns to write – or even invents the alphabet – to record his poems; again, I find this theory very attractive, except I would say for Homer, read Hesiod.

13. *'As to the age of Hesiod and Homer ... epic criticism'*: Pausanias, *Description of Greece*, 9.30.3.

14. *Hesiod's problematic Iron Age present in Works and Days*: The *Theogony* goes back to the beginning of time to trace the genealogy of the gods, but does so with a philosophical sweep that might well strike us as more modern than the anthropomorphizing quarrels among Homeric divinities. (Aristotle considered Hesiod a proto-philosopher rather than a poet.) Hesiod seems to believe in the gods' existence as supernatural forces, though, in a more literal way than the narrator of the Homeric epics.

15. *'the famous deeds of fighting heroes'*: *The Iliad*, trans. Robert Fagles (Harmondsworth: Penguin, 1990), p. 257.

16. *a stick*: While lyres remain the standard attribute of poets in classical times, other poetic 'sticks' do show up, such as the 'messenger stick' of poetry Pindar mentions in *Olympian* 6.91, or the rod in Archilochus' fragment 185.

17. *ingenious and relatively recent suggestion*: In a lecture by H. T. Wade-Gery, 'Hesiod', *Phoenix* 3(3) (1949), pp. 81–93.

18. *'a revolutionary gesture'*: Nassos Papalexandrou, 'Boiotian Tripods: The Tenacity of a Panhellenic Symbol in a Regional Context', *Hesperia* 77 (2008), pp. 251–82.

19. *one etymology of 'muse' connects them with towering places*: The etymology of 'muse' is contested – some connect it to the Proto-Indo-European (PIE) root *men* meaning 'mind', others to the PIE root *men* meaning 'mountain' or 'prominence'. See Boris Maslov, 'The Genealogy of the Muses: An Internal Reconstruction of Archaic Greek Metapoetics', *American Journal of Philology*, 137(3) (2016), pp. 411–46.

20. *the nativity story in the Gospel of St Luke*: Wade-Gery, 'Hesiod'. Coincidentally, St Luke, either a Hellenized Jew or Greek from Syria, is supposed to have died in Boeotia, where a chapel in Thebes contains some of his relics.

21. *'Hesiod thus detaches ... Homer'*: Charles Segal, *Singers, Heroes, and Gods in the Odyssey* (London: Cornell University Press, 1994), p. 140.

Further Reading

Athanassakis, Apostolos N. (ed. and trans.), *Hesiod: Theogony, Works and Days, Shield*, 2nd edn (Baltimore: Johns Hopkins University Press, 2004).

Hunter, Richard, *Hesiodic Voices: Studies in the Ancient Reception of Hesiod's Works and Days* (Cambridge: Cambridge University Press, 2014).

Janko, Richard, *Homer, Hesiod and the Hymns: Diachronic Development in Epic Diction* (Cambridge: Cambridge University Press, 1982).

Lamberton, Robert (ed.) and Stanley Lombardo (trans.), *Hesiod: Works and Days and Theogony* (Indianapolis/ Cambridge, Mass.: Hackett Publishing Company, 1993).

Lane Fox, Robin, *Travelling Heroes: Greeks and Their Myths in the Epic Age of Homer* (London: Allen Lane, 2008).

Lefkowitz, Mary R., *The Lives of the Greek Poets*, 2nd edn (Baltimore: Johns Hopkins University Press, 2012).

Montanari, F., A. Rengakos and C. Tsagalis (eds.), *Brill's Companion to Hesiod* (Leiden: Brill, 2009).

Most, Glenn W. (ed. and trans.), *Hesiod: Theogony, Works and Days, Testimonia*, Loeb Classical Library 57 (Cambridge, Mass./London: Harvard University Press, 2006).

Nagy, Gregory, 'Hesiod', in *Ancient Writers*, vol. 1, ed. T. J. Luce (New York: Scribner's, 1982), pp. 43–74.

Nagy, Gregory, *Greek Mythology and Poetics* (London: Cornell University Press, 1990).

Nelson, Stephanie, *God and the Land: The Metaphysics of Farming in Hesiod and Vergil. With a translation of Hesiod's Works and Days by David Grene* (Oxford: Oxford University Press, 1998).

Penglase, Charles, *Greek Myths and Mesopotamia: Parallels and Influence in the Homeric Hymns and Hesiod* (London: Routledge, 1994).

Powell, Barry B., *Homer and the Origin of the Greek Alphabet* (Cambridge: Cambridge University Press, 1991).

Powell, Barry B., *Writing: Theory and History of the Technology of Civilization* (West Sussex: Wiley-Blackwell, 2009).

Segal, Charles, *Singers, Heroes, and Gods in the Odyssey* (London: Cornell University Press, 1994).

Strauss Clay, Jenny, *Hesiod's Cosmos* (Cambridge: Cambridge University Press, 2003).

Tandy, David W., and Walter C. Neale, *Hesiod's Works and Days: A Translation and Commentary for the Social Sciences* (Berkeley, California: University of California Press, 1996).

Wade-Gery, H. T. 'Hesiod', *Phoenix* 3(3) (1949), pp. 81–93.

Wender, Dorothea (ed. and trans.), *Hesiod and Theognis* (Harmondsworth: Penguin, 1973).

West, Martin L., *Hesiod: Theogony. Edited with Prolegomena and Commentary* (Oxford: Clarendon Press, 1966).

West, Martin L., *Hesiod: Works and Days. Edited with Prolegomena and Commentary* (Oxford: Clarendon Press, 1978).

West, Martin L., *Hesiod: Theogony and Works and Days. A New Translation* (Oxford: Oxford University Press, 1988).

West, Martin L., *The East Face of Helicon: West Asiatic Elements in Greek Poetry and Myth* (Oxford: Clarendon Press, 1997).

Note on the Translation

> 'No race can prosper till it learns that there is as much
> dignity in tilling a field as in writing a poem.'
> – Booker T. Washington

When I first read Hesiod, as a student, and in translation,
the main impression I came away with was that he was a
crabbed old farmer, a misogynist, an archaism, a mytholo-
gist with none of the narrative verve of Homer, a wheezy
dispenser of old saws. He now fascinates me as a complex
figure, more misanthrope than misogynist, an original
thinker and proto-philosopher, with an unexpected streak
of generosity, lyricism and even (most surprisingly to me
this time around) a wry sense of humour. As I put it to a
classicist friend who had a similar reaction rereading him,
'Hesiod is a mensch.'

And he is recognizable and familiar as a poet: he lumps
poets in the same category of envious, begrudging guilds
as builders, potters and beggars. (The rivalry of potters in
classical Greece was proverbial; there is a famous example
of a potter, Euthymides, simultaneously boasting and
putting down another potter on a red-figure vase. The
inscription reads: 'Euphronius never made anything like
this'.) Being arguably the first poet to write his own 'bio'
in Western literature, Hesiod naturally emphasizes that
he is a prize-winner.

In short, I was won over by what Auden might call 'a

tone of voice, a personal speech'. Does it make sense to talk of Hesiod's voice? Some scholars would vehemently disagree, and say he is merely working in a tradition, dealing in ancient conventions, if there is even such a person we could call Hesiod. (See the Introduction.) Hesiod uses the same literary dialect as the Homeric epics, the *Iliad* and the *Odyssey*: Ionic Greek mixed with Aeolic; in Hesiod's case, with the odd Dorian or West Greek outlier. There are words, phrases and subjects, however, that are Hesiodic but not Homeric, and vice versa. One can argue this is a matter of genre, but these boundaries aren't as clear-cut as one might suppose: a martial epic like the *Iliad* can pause to describe in head-scratching detail the hitching up of a mule-drawn wagon, for instance, and a didactic farmer's guide can sing of the legends of heroes, titans and gods. Still there are things Hesiod would say, that Homer would not. Hesiod talks about himself (we know nothing of Homer), and we, or I anyway, believe him.

How to carry this over into English? What metre, what register, what tone, what diction? His voice, it seems to me, should be plain-spoken but not threadbare, to have a way with an aphorism and an argument, to be both stern and authoritative and personal and direct, to be scriptural at times and lyrical at others. He puts me in mind a little of Robert Frost, or at any rate I consider Frost the most Hesiodic of modern poets in English. Perhaps this seems a superficial comparison, both being poets who write verses about farming; but there are other affinities. Both are more sophisticated than they appear, wearing their considerable learning lightly. Both emphasize self-sufficiency ('Provide, Provide'), and take a dim view of the fallen modern world: Hesiod's Five Ages of Man, cascading from a Golden Age

to the current Age of Iron, is reflected in Frost's 'Nothing
Gold Can Stay'. For the ancients, Hesiod was the paragon
of the middle style; Frost is the excellent exemplar in
(American) English. 'Good fences make good neighbors',
the aphorism most people remember from Frost's poem
'Mending Wall', sounds as though it could have come
straight out of Hesiod. Frost's poem challenges this
received notion and mischievously imagines teasing his
neighbour into thought: '*Why* do they make good neigh-
bors? Isn't it / Where there are cows? . . .' I would maintain
that the setting is as much ancient Greece as modern New
England: the 'old-stone savage' at the end of the poem
could have walked straight out of the Five Ages of Man.
The Greek poet who is specifically concerned with neigh-
bours and the wandering-off of kine is of course Hesiod
of Askra:

> Who has a trusty neighbour, you'll allow,
> Has a share in something precious. Nary a cow
> Would be lost, but for bad neighbours . . .
>
> (346–8)

(Hesiod also assures us that a good neighbour is better
than kin, should there be an emergency on your prop-
erty; a fire, as I imagine it. A neighbour will rush over
half dressed, but the kinsman takes time to fasten his
belt.)

This is to say not that I am attempting to ventriloquize
Hesiod through Robert Frost; I hope this work comes
across simply as Hesiod in English; but I have taken Frost
as a model of the middle style in English, a way of working
in the vernacular that allows, as Hesiod's style does, for
archaism and the odd quaint or regional turn of phrase as

well as highfalutin' pronouncement. I have also taken the
occasional King James Biblical cadence, as Hesiod sounds
at times like an outraged Old Testament prophet. (This is
not entirely coincidental, as there is evidence that Hesiod
was conversant with aspects of Near Eastern thought and
culture.)

Hesiod composes his verses in unrhymed dactylic hexam-
eter, a limber six-foot line of between twelve and seventeen
syllables scanned according to a pattern of long and short.
That is to say, he writes in the exact same metre as Homer.
Six-beat lines in English, though, are famously ungainly and
sluggish. Alexander Pope describes and embodies the Eng-
lish alexandrine thus: 'That, like a wounded snake, drags its
slow length along.' Hexameters in English would have led to
some padding as well: Greek is polysyllabic, and swifter over
the same syllabic acreage than uninflected English, with its
Anglo-Saxon bent for monosyllables.

I ended up opting mainly for not-strictly-heroic couplets:
five-beat lines felt neither too long nor too short, even if this
sometimes meant telescoping the Greek, or at other times
letting the translator's holy grail, a 'line-by-line' corre-
spondence, slip through my fingers. (And of course there is
a long tradition in English of translating classical epic into
iambic pentameter.) The translation probably averages
about twelve lines, sometimes as many as fourteen, to every
ten of the original, line numbers in the text anchoring to the
Greek original. This means though that there are almost
always more than ten English lines within 'decades'.

While it might seem strange to introduce rhyme where
there is none (or next to none – there is a smattering of
atypical end-rhyme in the opening verses in the original),
for me, the rhymes serve both to carry the poem forwards,
much as the swinging 'shave-and-a-haircut' rhythm at

the end of each Greek line does, and give the English the flavour of aphorism: 'Early to bed, early to rise / Makes a man healthy, wealthy and wise.'

As a practitioner of rhyme and translation, I have found also that the added hurdle of rhyming lines, and of arranging lines so that the rhymes are on load-bearing words, has the benefit of making me work a little harder at trying to see the original clearly, looking at larger sections of text and their organization. I can't fudge through something puzzling if it must also rhyme and scan. Also, rhymed iambic pentameter couplets can have, in the twenty-first century, a slightly old-fashioned feel to them (although I suppose I am aiming for a timeless as opposed to antique diction), as Hesiod's Greek would have had a quaint ring even to classical authors.

In terms of the Greek text, I have largely followed the Oxford Classical Text edited by Friedrich Solmsen. For lines that are presumed to be interpolations, I have either indicated their excision or have translated them in square brackets. Occasionally I have chosen an alternative reading. (I can't say there was any method to this; I have proceeded largely according to poetic instinct.) In the case of lines 728–36, reordered in the OCT and many translations, I decided to see what happened if I just hewed to the line order as it is numbered in the manuscript tradition.

For the spelling of Greek words, I have tended to use a *k* instead of a *c* – Helikon, Kyme – but I am not entirely consistent (Cadmus, Calchis), not wishing to make certain words appear too unfamiliar.

As I first set out on translating the text, I was surprised to find Hesiod not only not antique and obsolete, but, with his concerns about justice and people's relationships with one another, the land and the divine, topical, even surprisingly contemporary. I have lived in Greece since 1999, and the scenario of siblings in a lawsuit over an inheritance is a commonplace. (Greece lacks a complete land registry, despite millions of euros allotted from the EU for this purpose.) Hesiod's coinage of 'dorophagoi' ('bribe-eaters') to describe the judges is instantly intelligible in modern Greek, in both language and cynicism. I even took, while working on the *Works and Days*, to describing Hesiod as though he were a contemporary poet I was translating, one living out in the boondocks of Boeotia, agitated about the corrupt government, in a lawsuit with his wastrel of a brother. Greeks would nod their heads in recognition.

During my work on the text, other words straight out of Hesiod's archaic Greek became more and more frequent in the newspapers as Greece's economic crisis hardened into a depression: debt (*chreos*), profit (*kerdos*), money (*chremata* – though 'money' per se did not yet exist in Hesiod's Greece), trial/lawsuit (*dike*). Staggering debt (government books cooked with the collusion of Goldman Sachs), brazen corruption, iron-hearted austerity measures (not to mention bank closures, capital controls, record unemployment), all made it feel as though we were late in the Ages of Man. When Hesiod says: 'I would not be an honest man, not now, / Nor wish it for my son – when I see how / It's evil to be honest in a land / Where crooks and schemers have the upper hand' (270–72), he seemed to be speaking to the present moment, and for the average Greek citizen. In Athens, a number of the city's inhabitants, having lost the jobs that connected them to urban life, as well as many young people with no prospects, decided to return to ancestral villages and make a go of working neglected olive groves and fields.

Even the seemingly throw-away bit of autobiography, that Hesiod's father was an economic migrant from Asia Minor (from a town on the coast just south of Lesbos), who sailed across the Aegean to settle and start a new life on the mainland, seemed to be plucked out of the news-cast, as displaced peoples poured into Greece along the exact same migration and trade-routes that interconnected the Bronze and Iron Age cultures of the Mediterranean.

Midway through the translation, my family and I set out on a road trip from Athens to Askra, about a two-hour drive: modern 'Askri' (not quite on the site of ancient Askra, Hesiod's hometown, but close enough, at the foot of Mount Helikon and the Valley of the Muses), in mid-September, almost exactly at the date, according to the constellations, that Hesiod says the grapes should be harvested. Driving through modern Thebes, still Boeotia's most populous town, an unprepossessing place jostling with cement apart-ment blocks, hardware stores, streets clogged with automobile traffic, lorries, and tractors, one already began to get the sense of a place that was 'Bad in winter, harsh in summer, not / Ever pleasant' (640). Arabic script over a cheap sandwich shop that catered to migrant workers reminded me with a shock that Cadmus, the legendary founder of the city, had brought into Greece the 'Phoenician' letters that would become the Greek alphabet. (Ritsona, near Thebes, is now the site of a refugee camp, the residents themselves perhaps arriving via places not far from Cadmus' birthplace, ancient Tyre, in modern Lebanon.)

But Askri is further afield, and maybe longer ago, a footnote of a town at the base of Mount Helikon, a clus-ter of houses, a couple of coffee shops (the *kafeneion* in modern Greece serving much the purpose of the black-smith's shop in *Works and Days*, a place for men to procrastinate, pontificate and shoot the breeze – shall we imagine that in Hesiod's time there was even a hot beverage on offer?), a tavern or two; a butcher, a baker, a little plaza dedicated to the Muses Nine, with a bust of Hesiod, native son, presiding at one end. Naturally, the ancient Greek inscribed on the plinth is not the famous put-down of Askra ('Bad in winter' etc.), but the more industrious 'There's no shame / In working, but in shirking, much to blame' (311). The road swarmed with tractors and wagons – though not wagons anyone had had to fangle himself, out of a hundred timbers and baffling measurements – piled precariously high with grapes from the harvest. The streets swam with the juice of crushed grapes, and the air shimmered and thrummed with must-inebriated bees.

Many of these grapes were grown on the slope of Mount Helikon in the Valley of the Muses itself; one of the varieties, 'Mouchtaro', a Turkish word meaning 'elected chief of the village' – perhaps the ancient Greek translation would be 'Basileús' – unique to the valley, was made into a dark, no, almost black, wine by a local winery known as the Estate of the Nine Muses. (We went by to talk to the vintners, and they confessed that they had tried to harvest and press grapes exactly in accordance with Hesiod's instructions, but the results had been disappointing.) The town of Askri was, appropriately, uninspiring, prosaic, work-a-day; but a quick drive out into the valley itself, in gold afternoon light canted over the mountains, among purple wildflowers and Muse-haunted groves, offered us an enchantment that was ancient, ephemeral and everywhere. It's a good place for a tripod and a shrine.

Acknowledgements

I would like to thank the following poets, scholars and translators for their generous assistance, their encouragement and feedback, sharp eyes and keen ears, thumbs up and thumbs down. I started this project as a translator, and found myself in a thicket of scholarship and in need of guidance. Many a felicity, correction and insight is owed to the following, while I acknowledge all errors, outlandish fancies and stubborn wrongheadedness as mine own: Apostolos N. Athanassakis, James Campbell, Chris Childers, Nancy Felson, Rachel Hadas, Richard Jenkyns, Brady Kiesling, Stephanie Larson, Mike Levine, Jim McCue, Peter McDonald, Dimitri Nakassis, Robin Osborne, John Papadopoulos, Yannis Petropoulos, Angela Taraskiewicz, Philip J. Thibodeau.

Peter Carson first set me an the path of translating *Works and Days* but did not live to see the end result. I miss his cool editorial eye and warm encouragement.

I am grateful to Ben Folit-Weinberg, who assisted in things poetic, classical, and practical with Hesiodic diligence.

Thank you also to the journals *Able Muse*, *The Hopkins Review* and *The New Criterion* for printing short passages of the translation in process.

And thanks also always to John Psaropoulos, who has endured many works and days with me in the hardscrabble field of Hesiod, and who drove me to Askra to see the grape harvest and the Valley of the Muses.

I would like to dedicate the translation to Jason and Atalanta. May they look back from a better future than we can predict, and view these troubled times as an Iron Age.

A. E. S., Athens, Greece, March 2017

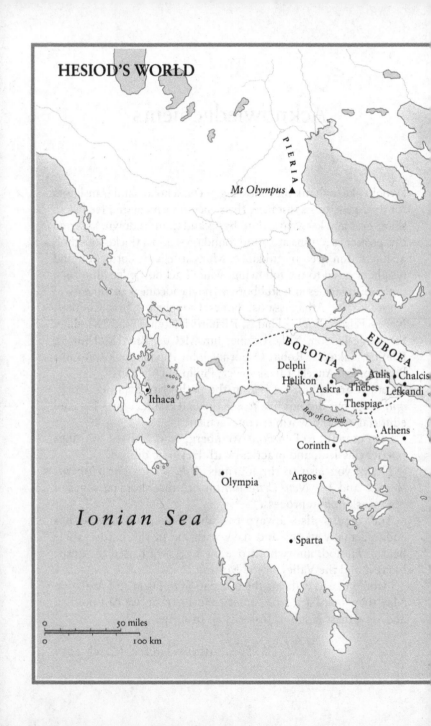

HESIOD'S WORLD

PIERIA

Mt Olympus ▲

BOEOTIA

EUBOEA

Delphi
Helikon   Aulis   Chalcis
          Askra Thebes
Ithaca   Thespiae Lefkandi

Bay of Corinth

Athens

Corinth

Argos

Olympia

Ionian Sea

Sparta

0   50 miles
0   100 km

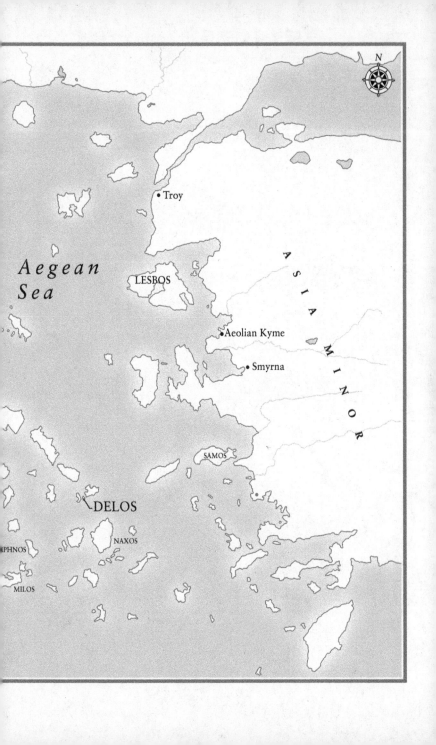

WORKS AND DAYS

MUSES from Pieria, whose song is fame,
Come. Hymn your father Zeus, through whom a name
Is won by mortal men, on every tongue,
Or through whose mighty will they go unsung
In anonymity. With ease he makes
The weak man strong, with ease the strong he breaks,
He brings forth the obscure, he levels the great,
He withers the tall, and makes the crooked straight.
Hear me, Sky-shaker, You who dwell on high,
With justice put our laws to rights, while I
Tell Perses the plain truths to steer him by.   10

It turns out Strife's a twin, a double birth –
There are, not one, but *two* Strifes on the earth –[1]
A man who gets to know them both admits
One's blessed, one's cursed – the two are opposites.
One brings forth discord, nurtures evil war:
Wicked, there's nothing mortals love her for,
But the gods have willed men honour her, despite
Her dragging weight; the other, Shady Night
Gave birth to first. This Strife, high-seated Zeus
Set in earth's roots – for this one has a use:
She spurs a man who otherwise would shirk,   20

Shiftless and lazy, to put his hands to work
Seeing a rich man plough and plant and labour
To set up house – then neighbour envies neighbour
Racing to reach prosperity. This Strife
Is boon to man. And that's why in this life
Potter hates potter, builder has no regard
For builder, nor beggar, beggar; bard loathes bard.[2]

Perses, take this to heart, lest Strife, whose quirk
Is mischief-making, draw your mind from work;
And, eavesdropping in the marketplace, you waste
30   Your time spying on quarrels. For a taste
For feuds and assemblies should be in short supply
For one who has not laid some ripe grain by
Under his roof to live on – a good year's worth
Of Demeter's spires of corn, born of the earth.
When you've a surplus, you can cook up trouble
Over another's property. No double
Chance for you: let's settle this fair and square –
Straight judgements are from Zeus and past compare.
Already we've divvied up our lots, but you
Keep laying hold of more than is your due,
Bearing great honours to those gift-guzzling kings[3]
40   Who mean to pass this judgement. Foolish things,
They don't know 'half's more wholesome' – or how well
Mallow sustains; how filling, asphodel.[4]

For the gods have hidden livelihood away
From men, else you could work a single day
And easily have enough for living clear
Without a lick of work for the whole year,
And soon season the rudder over the smoke,
Retire the drudging mules, the oxen's yoke.

But Zeus hid it away, galled in his heart[5]
That he'd been duped by Prometheus' wry art,[6]
So he invented dismal woes for men
And hid fire – which Prometheus again   50
Filched in a hollow fennel stalk – a plunder
From under the nose of Zeus who joys in thunder.

And Zeus, cloud-herder, spoke with words of bile:
'Iapetus' son, exceeding all in guile,
You're glad you pilfered fire, and tricked my mind:
So much the worse for you and all mankind
To come: I'll pay them back evil for fire,
Evil in which they find their heart's desire;
They'll greet their bane with open arms!' Then after
The sire of men and gods thundered with laughter,
He ordered famed Hephaestus without delay   60
To moisten earth with water, and give the clay
A human's speech and strength, the lovely face
Of a deathless goddess, a virgin's form and grace;
He bade Athena make her a dab hand
At weaving intricate cloth, and his command
To golden Aphrodite was to shed
Beauty and troublous passion on her head,
And limb-wasting worries. Then Argus-killer
Hermes the Go-between, Zeus told to fill her
With a bitch's mind and the cunning of a thief.

He spoke, and all the gods obeyed their chief.
To Zeus's plan, the Cripple[7] right away   70
Modelled a modest maiden out of clay;
Clear-eyed Athena dressed her, cinched her waist,
And Lady Sweet-talk and the Graces placed
Gold jewels upon her, and the fair-tressed Hours

Wreathed her all about with springtime flowers,
And Athena fitted adornment to each part.

Then Hermes Argus-killer set in her heart
Lies and wheedling words, a knack for deceit.
The design of Zeus deep-thunderer complete,
Hermes, the gods' herald and proclaimer,
80 Gave her a voice. 'Pandora' he would name her,
The 'All-endowed', since all with an abode
On Mount Olympus had some gift bestowed
Upon her – grief for all bread-winning men.

When Hermes had done this feat of treachery, then
Father Zeus sent him, Argus-killer, swift
Messenger of the Gods, with her as gift
To 'Hindsight' (Epimetheus). And though 'Forethought'
(Prometheus) had warned him, he forgot
To send back, not accept, a gift from Zeus
Lest evil come to man. It was no use:
The deed was done before he understood
That what he had accepted was no good.

90 For once the tribes of men lived on the soil
Untouched by woe, apart from parlous toil,
And free from Man's destruction, dread disease.
[Affliction ages men quick as you please.]⁸
But *woman* grappled off the jar's huge lid,⁹
Scattering its contents as she did,
Unleashing sorry troubles on Mankind.
Hope only did not fly. She stayed behind
In her impregnable home beneath the lip
Of the jar; before she had a chance to slip
Out, woman closed the lid, as Zeus designed.

More ills galore go roving through Mankind: 100
The sea is full of bane, the earth of blight,
Some ailments come by day, and some by night,
Bringing men ills, they roam of their own choice;
In silence, since Zeus robbed them of their voice:
No getting round it, Zeus's schemes prevail.

If you like, I shall sum up another tale –
I'll tell it well and true – take it to heart:
How gods and mortals spring from the same start.

The first race of humanity[10] was Gold;
The Olympian gods created it of old,   110
In the time of Kronos, when he ruled the air.
Like gods they lived, with spirits free from care;
And grim old age never encroached. The feast
Where they moved limbs to music never ceased;
Their hands and feet not ageing in the least.
They were free from every evil you could number,
And when death came, it stole on them like slumber.
They had good things galore; a bumper yield
Of corn sprung volunteering from the field.
They shared the harvest, peaceful as you please,
And gentle, willing, dwelt in bounteous ease.
[Loved by the gods, their sheep crowding the fold.][11]   120
When earth had covered up this race of Gold,
As spirits[12] they remained, by Zeus's will;
Benevolent, they move among us still,
Guardians who keep watch over men,
All justice and all crimes lie in their ken,
Shrouded with mist, they walk abroad in stealth;
Within their gift, the kingly boon of wealth.

The second race the gods made was by far
Inferior, a Silver Race, on par
In neither brains nor brawn: each child would cling,
130   Great baby, to his mother's apron string
A century, playing house. And when in time
They came to puberty and reached their prime,
They didn't live for long at all; instead
Their reckless acts of folly left them dead.
They had no self-control, could not restrain
Themselves from wreaking outrages and pain
On one another, and counted among their vices
Neglect of the gods, the rightful sacrifices
That men perform, as custom says they must;
And then Zeus hid these also in disgust
Because they would not give the gods their due.
140   And so the ground has covered this race too;
And though they were inferior in worth,
Yet they are blessed shades beneath the earth,
Honour attends them still.

                                    Then in their place
Zeus the Father forged a Brazen Race
Of men worse than the Silver; terrible, fierce
And tough as ash-wood for the hafts of spears:
War was their work – they loved the work of war –
The doleful deeds, the violence, the gore.
They ate no bread. Their hearts were hard as stone.
No one could touch them, for their might had grown
Along with their limbs. All weapons they would wield
Were bronze, their roofs were bronze, they worked
150   the field
With tools of bronze, black iron unknown. They fell
At one another's hands to draughty Hell,

Nameless, for all their fearsomeness, undone
By death, snatched from the bright light of the sun.

And when the ground had covered up this race
In turn, Zeus made a fourth one on the face
Of the richly pasturing earth, a juster one
And better, a god-like race of heroes known
As demi-gods – the race that came before   160
Our own on the boundless earth. These, wicked war
And the baneful battle-din laid low, one band
At seven-gated Thebes, in Cadmus-land,
Wrangling over Oedipus's sheep,[13]
And others who sailed across the salty deep
To Troy, for Helen of the lovely hair.[14]
And some death's destiny has buried there;
But others Zeus has settled near the tide   170
Of deep-swirled Ocean, to thrive there and abide
Far off from men – with spirits undistressed,
At the earth's ends, on Islands of the Blessed,
Happy heroes, for whom sweet fruits appear
And the fields yield their bounty thrice a year.

[Away from gods. Kronos rules them. Zeus,   173a
The father of men and gods, had set him loose,
And now and for ever, he holds an honoured place,
As is meet, and Zeus has set another race
Of men in turn upon earth's bounteous face.][15]

Would I were not among the Fifth. I'm torn:
Would I be better dead or not yet born? –
For this age is an Iron Age indeed –
Suffering never ceases for our breed:

By day, men toil; night worries them with care,
And the gods will give them troubles hard to bear;
But even so, some good things will alloy
180   Their lot of woe. And still, Zeus will destroy
This race, when babes are born already grey
At the temples, and when father in no way
Shall share a bond with sons, nor sons with father,
Nor guest with host, nor comrades with each other,
Nor brother love his brother as before;
Soon men won't honour parents any more
But will heap insults on old age – they'll learn
About the payback of the gods in turn –
Ingrates for their own rearing. Lacking pity,
With the rule of fist, one sacks another's city.
190   Thankless will be the man who keeps his word,
The good and the just. The wicked will be preferred
In honour, outrageous men who take the law
In their own hands, and there shall be no Awe.
The bad will harm the good; he won't be loath
To twist his words, and seal them with an oath.
And spiteful Envy, with her evil eye[16]
And acid tongue, will keep herself close by
To every miserable man, while Awe
And Retribution will indeed withdraw,
Abandoning mankind and the broad roads
Of earth, for the Olympian abodes
Of the Deathless Ones, veiling themselves in white
And hiding the beauty of their skin from sight.
200   Dismal troubles will be left behind:
No deliverance from evil for mankind.

Now I shall tell a fable to the Kings,
Who have the wit to understand such things:
Thus did the hawk address the nightingale[17]
With her speckled throat, as he began to sail
Up to the clouds, clutching her in his claws,
While she lamented piteously because
His talons pierced her: from his haughty beak
He said, 'Good madam, why is it you shriek?
You're in a greater's power. You have no choice
But go where I take you, despite your lovely voice,
And if I wish, I shall make you my dinner
Or set you free. The fool will be no winner:
Who strives with stronger has himself to blame   210
For losing, and adds suffering to shame.'
Thus spoke the long-winged hawk, the swift of flight.

So Perses, you be heedful of what's right;
Don't nurture Arrogance – she's a disaster
For lowly mortals; she will overmaster
Even noble men and crush them with her load
Once they encounter troubles. The better road
Is the one bypassing Arrogance to wend
To Justice; Justice triumphs in the end.
The fool learns this the hard way, for Oath hunts
Down crooked verdicts, dogging them at once,
And when Justice is dragged away to court   220
By swallowers of bribes, who make a sport
Of judgements, there's an outcry. Then she'll hide
Herself in mist, and roam where men abide,
Weeping through the city, and bringing trouble
To those who drove her out and who deal double.
But when men deal in justice straight and fair
Alike to citizen and foreigner

And do not overstep law or presume,
Their city flourishes, their people bloom,
Then Peace, who rears young men, on earth holds sway,
And Zeus, far-seer, keeps cruel War at bay.
230 Famine and folly pass the righteous by:
The just feast on what well-worked fields supply.
The earth abounds for them: the mountain oak
Is acorn-crowned, and bee-filled, for such folk.[18]
Their sheep are heavy-laden with wool. Their wives
Bear children that favour fathers. Throughout their lives
They bloom with blessings. They need never sail:
The land provides for them and does not fail.

But Zeus marks evil-doers, who sow seeds
Of pride, and punishes their wicked deeds.
240 And often a whole city pays the price
For one bad man's outrageousness and vice.
Zeus son of Kronos rains down woe like weather
Out of the sky, hunger and plague together.
Men die. Wives don't give birth. Households reduce
According to the will of Olympian Zeus.
At other times, he mows broad armies down,
Or levels walls, or makes armadas drown.
So Judges, mind this judgement: understand
The deathless ones are always close at hand
250 Marking those crooked judges who have trod
On others, heedless men who fear no god.
Thrice myriad, the Watchers of Mankind
On the rich earth, the deathless host who find
Out crimes and judgements. They roam everywhere
Across the land, invisible as air.

There is a maiden, Justice, child of Zeus,
Revered by the gods. When men play fast and loose
With her good name, then straight away she flies
To Daddy's side and tells him of their lies,   260
Until the city's people make amends
For those who twisted justice to their ends,
Heedless. Judges, you gift-gluttons, beware:
Drop crooked verdicts, speak them fair and square.
He harms himself who harms another man;
The plotter is the worst hurt by the plan.

The eye of Zeus sees all; all it surveys
It understands, nothing escapes his gaze.
And if he likes, he looks within a town,
And knows the sort of judgement handed down.
I would not be an honest man, not now,   270
Nor wish it for my son – when I see how
It's evil to be honest in a land
Where crooks and schemers have the upper hand.
I still have hopes this isn't what Zeus planned.

So Perses, mull these matters in your mind,
Give ear to Justice; leave Force far behind.
For Kronos' son gave justice to mankind;
The fish and beasts and winged birds of the air
Eat one another – they don't have a share
Of law and right – he made the law for man,
And this way is by far the better plan.
Far-seeing Zeus will grant prosperity
To him who speaks up for the truth, but he   280
Who bears false witness and lies under oath,
Injures past healing law and good name both,
And his descendants live under a cloud;
The sons of one true to his word are proud.

Fool Perses, what I say's for your own good.
Bad's had for the taking, woes galore,
The road is smooth and short – she lives next door.
The strait and narrow path the gods have set
290 To Virtue is steep and long, and paved with sweat.
It's hard going at first, but by the time
You reach the peak, it seems an easy climb
Uphill as it is.
                    That man is best
Who thinks for himself, and puts all to the test
To weigh the ends and outcomes. It will suffice
Even to heed another's good advice.
But he who can't think for himself, nor once
Learn from another, is a useless dunce.

Take what I've said to heart. Start taking pains,
O Perses! Noble blood runs through your veins! [19]
Work keeps the wolf of famine from the door;
300 Well-crowned Demeter[20] smiles and fills your store.
But famine dogs the heels of those who shirk,
And men and gods shun him who will not work –
He's like blunt-bottomed drones who take their ease
While gobbling up the labour of the bees.
Look to your work, order your chores with reason,
So that barns groan with harvest in due season.
It's work that prospers men, and makes them rich
[310 In heads of livestock, and it's working which
excised] Endears you to the immortals. There's no shame
In working, but in shirking, much to blame.
And if you work, the man who twiddles his thumbs
Is quick to envy you grown rich. Wealth comes
With fame and honour in her retinue.

With work, you better what's allotted you.
Don't covet the possessions of your neighbour:
Turn your foolish heart. Look to your labour,
I urge you, to secure your living – heed:
Shame's no provider for the man in need,
Shame who can harm a man or make him grand.
For Shame and poverty go hand in hand;
Bold goes with riches. Property should not   320
Be up for grabs. God-given's better got.
For if somebody seizes some great prize
With force of arms, or burgles with his lies,
As often happens when greed tricks the mind
And brazen Shamelessness leaves Shame behind,
The gods with ease obscure him: all he reaps
Is a dwindled house; wealth isn't his for keeps.
The same for him who wrongs a guest or harms
A suppliant, or takes into his arms
His brother's wife behind his brother's back,[21]
Indecent deed! or him who in his lack
Of scruples swindles orphans, or in rage   330
At his father on the cruel sill of age
Hurls bruising words at him; that man's abhorred
By Zeus himself, and reaps his just reward.

But turn your witless mind from all such vice.
According to your means, make sacrifice[22]
With a clean, right spirit, to the gods, and burn
Bright thigh-bones on the altar, and in turn
Give votives and libations, both at night
And at the first return of holy light,
So heaven smiles on you and your affairs,   340
And none bids for your land, but you for theirs.

Invite a friend but not a foe to feast –
Invite the man close by not last nor least;
If something bad should happen on your farm,
Neighbours arrive half-dressed at the alarm;
Kinsmen, belted. A bad neighbour's a curse
As a good one is a treasure – nothing's worse.
Who has a trusty neighbour, you'll allow,
Has a share in something precious. Nary a cow
Would be lost, but for bad neighbours. Keep good track
When you measure from your neighbour, pay him back
350 Good measure too, better if in your power;
You'll find him steadfast in a needful hour.

Don't profit wickedly. Ill-gotten gains
Amount to nothing more than woes and banes.
Befriend a friend, go meet the man who'll meet you.
Give to a giver; don't to one who'll cheat you.
Give begets gift, grasp: grudge. For Give is breath
While Seize is evil, and her wages, death.
Who gives with open hands, though great the gift,
Rejoices in it and his spirits lift.
But he who steals, trusting in brazen vice,
360 Though small the theft, congeals his heart to ice.

Deposit even small amounts, but do
It often, and you'll find that they accrue.
He wards off sun-scorched famine who can add
To what he has. To store at home's not bad;
Outside is risky. To take from what you've got
Is fine, to be in need of what you've not
Is woe to the spirit. Mind you, that's how things are.

Drink deep from new-broached or from near-drained jar.
Thrift's for halfway, but stingy at the end.
Ensure a settled payment for your friend;   370
Smile on a brother, but have a witness, when
Trust and mistrust alike have ruined men.

Don't let a woman mystify your mind
With sweet talk and the sway of her behind –
She's just after your barn. He who believes
A woman, is a man who trusts in thieves.
May an only son shore up his father's walls,
For that's how wealth amasses in the halls.
May he die full of years and leave one heir,
An only son in turn, though Zeus might spare
Untold wealth on bigger numbers – more
Hands, more chores done, and a fuller store.   380
But if it's wealth you long for in your chest,
Then do this: work on work and never rest.

When Atlas' daughters rise,[23] the Pleiades,
Start harvesting, plough at their setting.[24] These
Are hidden forty days and forty nights.
But as the year goes round, once more their lights
Appear, and then it's time to hone iron tools.
For plains- and coastal-dwellers, the same rules
Apply, for those who live far from the swells
Of the sea, and those who live in glens and dells,   390
Rich country. Naked sow and naked plough
And reap your harvest naked,[25] this is how
You'll gather all Demeter's works in season,
Ripe in due time, and so there'll be no reason
For you to beg in vain from door to door
As you've come to me now. I'll give no more,

No extra. No-count Perses – Work! Again,
Work at the work gods have marked out for men
Lest sick at heart, with wife and kids, you find
400 You beg from neighbours and they pay no mind.
You might get handouts twice, three times, but four?
Don't waste your breath by pestering once more,
Your words broadcast in vain. I'd urge you heed:
Think how to clear debts and not starve. You'll need
A woman and an ox to start a life:
A ploughing ox; bondswoman, not a wife,
One who can follow oxen, and prepare
The household's needs and management with care,
Lest you go begging and be turned away,
And fruits of your labour dwindle day by day.
410 Don't put off till tomorrow or till later –
No barn is filled by a procrastinator.
Through diligence, the harvest yield redoubles;
The shirker's always wrestling with troubles.

When the fierce sun restrains his scorching powers,
And mighty Zeus sends down autumnal showers,
Then man's skin feels the lightness of relief,
Then searing Sirius's time by day is brief
Hanging above the heads of doom-fed men
And takes a greater share of night – that's when
420 Wood's least worm-riddled, and the trees you chop
Cease sprouting shoots, and let their foliage drop.
That's when the time is ripe for cutting wood:
Cut three feet for a mortar; three cubits' good
For pestles; for an axle, a seven-foot
Length (eight for a mallet-head to boot).
That's how things are well-fitted, part to part:
Cut three-span fellies to make a ten-palm cart.[26]

Timbers often curve, so keep an eye
Out for a natural plough-tree; when you spy
Such timber made of holm oak as you roam
The mountains and the fields, then bring it home:
For ox-drawn-ploughing, holm-oak's strength's
    unmatched
Once Athena's henchman[27] has attached   430
The plough-tree to the stock with pegs and fit
The other end to the pole and fastened it.
Equip your household with two ploughs, take care
To have a single-piece one, and a spare
Well joined. It's better – that way if you broke
One plough, you'd have another one to yoke
The oxen to. Elm poles are sturdiest
Or laurel, oak for stocks, while holm is best
For trees. Go get two bullocks in their prime
At nine years old, their strength unsapped by time.
That team is best for work. They will not wrangle
In the furrow with each other so they mangle
The plough, the botched job left mid-field. A strong,   440
Hale forty-year-old man should follow along,[28]
Who's breakfasted on a quarter loaf-of-eight,[29]
And knows his job, and makes his furrow straight,
Mind on his work, not looking any longer
To his age-mates; another, no whit younger,
To sow, not over-seed: a young man tends
To flightiness, distracted by his friends.

Be mindful when you hear the clanging cry
Of the crane migrating through the cloudy sky,[30]
She brings the sign for ploughing and the start   450
Of winter rains – her cry eats at the heart

Of the man who's oxenless. This season calls
For battening curved-horned oxen in their stalls.
To say, 'Lend me a cart and team,' is easy –
'*They've work at home*': refusal's just as breezy.
The man whose wealth's all in his head will say
He'll make a cart, the fool, when there's no way:
The boards that make a wagon are five score:
Be wise, lay up your hundred boards before.

When first the opportunity to plough
Shows itself to mortals, that means *now*:
Jump to it, both you and your slaves together,
460 Plough dry and wet, according to the weather;
Be brisk at dawn, so your fields fill with yield.
Springtime's when to turn the soil. A field
Left fallow in the summer is just right:
Sow the fallow while the soil's still light.
Fallow is child-charmer, famine-cheater.

Pray to the Zeus Below and chaste Demeter
That Demeter's sacred grain grow ripe and bow
With heaviness, as you set hand to plough
Right at the start of tilling, and you switch
The backs of oxen tugging at the hitch
That pulls the yoke pole. Let a slave make toil
470 For birds by covering the seeds with soil,
Following with a mattock close behind.
Good husbandry is best for humankind,
Bad management's the worst. This way is sound,
And grain will bend with fullness to the ground.
And if Zeus grant you bring a fine yield in,
You'll brush the cobwebs from the storage bin,

And I'd say you'll be glad to have your stores
Of livelihood at hand, within your doors.
And you'll be prosperous come silver Spring,
And you won't envy others anything;
But another will entreat you in his dearth.

If you begin to plough the holy earth
At winter solstice, you'll reap squatting down   480
Covered in dust, and binding, with a frown,
Scant handfuls, ears and stalks at either end,
A basket's worth. Nothing to recommend
Yourself to others. But the mind of Zeus
Is, to mortals' ken, a thing abstruse,
Different at different times. Yet if you till
Too late, there is a remedy even still
When first the cuckoo cuckoos in the oak,[31]
On the boundless earth, delighting mortal folk,
If at that time Zeus rains three days, not stopping,
Just filling an ox-hoof-print, not overtopping.
That's how Late-plougher vies with Early-start.   490
Note everything and mark it in your heart,
Let nothing slip your notice, not the hour
Of silver Spring's approach, nor timely shower.

In winter, pass the blacksmith's forge, don't stop
Where men gather and chat in his warm shop.
When cold keeps men from toiling in the fields,
One who is diligent may boost his yields,
Lest you get caught in winter's bitter freeze
By Shiftlessness with Poverty, and squeeze
Your swollen foot[32] with a bony hand. The dope
Who's idle and awaits an empty hope,

Gripes in his soul, lacking a livelihood.
500 But as provider, Hope is not much good,
Not to a man who lacks his daily bread
But loiters at the forge all day instead.
Instruct your slaves while summer's in its prime:
'Summer won't last. Build shelter while there's time.'

Lenaion – the entire month – is rife
With evils, each day like a skinning knife.
Avoid it, and the killing frosts brought forth
Upon the earth when wind blows from the north,
Through Thrace, mother of horses, and sets seething
The wide sea. Wold and wood howl with its breathing.
Falling on crowds of lofty oaks and dense
Groves of fir, in the mountain dales, it bends
510 Them down to the rich earth; the whole wood wails.
The creatures shiver, and they tuck their tails
Under their genitals; no matter how thick
Their fur, the wind's cold cuts right to the quick.
It pierces ox-hide, useless as a coat,
And blows right through the long hair of a goat.
But the force of the North Wind won't blow through
    sheep –
Their woolly fleeces grow too thick and deep.
It sends an old man rolling head over heels.[33]
Indoors, the soft-skinned virgin never feels
520 The cold, snug by her mother, ignorant of
(At least as yet) the deeds of golden Love,
And takes a bath, and oils her tender skin
Richly with ointments, and lies down within,
On a winter's day, when Sans-a-bone,[34] in gloom,
Gnaws at his foot down in his fireless room,

Since the sun leads him to no new pasture then;
It roams among the cities of black men,
And among the Greeks is slower peeping out.[35]
Then woodland-dwellers, with horns and without,
Miserably, with teeth a-chatter, rush,   530
Crashing pell-mell through the underbrush,
Shelter is the only thing they crave:
They seek a sturdy lair, protected cave.
That's when they shuffle down the woodland track
Like a man on three legs with a broken back,[36]
His head bowed, gaze fixed on the ground below;
Just so they rove, shunning the blank of snow.

You also should seek shelter from exposure:
Soft cloak, and full-length tunic for enclosure,
Thick weft, fine warp, and wrap your body tight,
So you don't shake and hairs don't stand upright,   540
And bind your feet in snug boots of ox leather,
Well-made, lined with thick felt. When winter weather
Has come, stitch skins of firstling kids together[37]
With thongs of ox sinew, so you can drape
Your shoulders with a rain-resistant cape.
You'll need a well-made felted hat to set
Up top to keep your ears from getting wet,
For dawn is chill when the North Wind befalls,
Mist stretched down from the starry skies appalls
The fruited fields of blessed men, mist drifted
Up from the ever-flowing streams, and lifted   550
High above the ground by a gust. At close
Of day, sometimes it rains, sometimes it blows
When the North Wind comes stampeding out of Thrace
Driving thick clouds – finish your tasks, and race

Back home ahead of him, so you don't get
Caught in a fog, skin soaked, clothes sopping wet.
Avoid this – for this wintry month is worst,
A hard month on the herds, to man accursed.
Put oxen on half-rations then, but give
A man a little more on which to live,[38]
560   For that's when nights are long, nights who are kind[39]
And bring us respite. Year's end,[40] keep this in mind,
Balancing night and day, when Mother Earth
Once more brings all her many fruits to birth.

Sixty winter days beyond the year's
Turning is when Arcturus first appears,[41]
Rising out of the Ocean's sacred stream,
And at the point of dusk will brightly gleam.
Next, the swallow, Pandion's child, will wing[42]
Into sight, dawn-weeper, harbinger of Spring.[43]
570   Best prune your vines, beat her while you've a chance.
But when house-hauler[44] clambers up the plants
From the ground, fleeing the Pleiades, forget
Hoeing your vines. Now rouse your slaves and whet
Your scythes. Shun shady spots and lying in
Till dawn at harvest, when sun withers the skin.
No time to waste now, get your crop inside.
Rise early, so the harvest will provide.
One-third of work is Dawn's own share to ask,
Dawn lights the path, Dawn offers you the task,
580   Dawn shows herself, and sets men on their way;
Dawn yokes the oxen at the break of day.

When thistle blooms, and loud Cicada rings[45]
In a tree, and shrills from underneath his wings
Clear, ceaseless song, in toilsome summertime,
That's when she-goats are fattest, wine is prime,
Women are lustiest, and men instead
Are at their weakest, parched in knees and head
By Sirius,[46] and the heat's made their skin dry.
Then let there be a shady rock nearby,
And Bibline wine,[47] some good baked bread to eat,   590
Cheese from goats just drying up, some meat
From a forest-browsing cow with never a calf
And also meat from firstling kids. Then quaff
Some fire-bright wine stretched in that shady place.
And when you've had your fill and turned your face
Into the fresh West Wind, make offering
From an ever-flowing, clear, untroubled spring:
Pour three parts water to one part of wine.

And when mighty Orion starts to shine,[48]
Urge slaves to thresh Demeter's holy corn
On a threshing floor that's airy and well worn.
Then store it in jars in measure well and good.   600
When you've laid by all of your livelihood
Under your roof, then turn your hired man out,
And seek a weaver girl, one who's without
A child. A girl who has a brat beneath
Her feet's no good. And get a dog, with teeth,
Sharp teeth, and don't begrudge the hound a meal,
Lest some day-sleeping man break in and steal
Your things. And gather hay and straw inside
So your oxen and your mules are well supplied.
Then let slaves[49] ease their knees, unyoke your team.

And when Orion and Sirius both gleam
610 Mid-sky, and when Dawn with her rosy fingers
Looks on Arcturus,[50] make sure no cluster lingers
On the vine, Perses. See that the grapes are laid
In the sun ten days and nights, five in the shade.
On the sixth day, draw the vintage into jars,
Boon of glad Dionysus. When the stars
Of the Pleiades, Hyades, and Orion sink,
That's when it is again high time to think
Of ploughs. Let the year be fitted to the soil.

But if a yearning seizes you to roil
620 In stormy seamanship, when the Pleiades,
Fleeing Orion, sink in cloudy seas,
That's when all kinds of wind blasts rage. Don't keep
Your ship any longer on the wine-dark deep,
But work the earth, and mind what I command:
Now's when to draw your ship up on dry land,
And pile stones round to keep wet winds at bay.
Pull out its bilge-plug, that it not decay
With Zeus's rainfall. Stow the gear, all things
You need for sailing, making sure the wings[51]
Of your seaworthy ship are in good trim.
And hang the well-wrought rudder in the scrim
630 Of smoke. Till sailing season comes, just wait.
Then drag your swift ship seawards. Range the freight
In its hold, get ready for the profit you'll
Bring home – just like our father – you great fool,
Perses! – our father, mine and yours, who, failing
A better living, took up ships and sailing.
He came here in his black ship over the sea,
Forsaking Aeolian Kyme, so he might flee,
Not wealth nor riches nor prosperity

But Evil Need, Zeus-given. He settled down
Near Helikon, in Askra, wretched town,
Bad in winter, harsh in summer, not   640
Ever pleasant. But you, Perses, take thought
Of the ripe time for the task, and most of all
For seafaring. With boats, admire the small,
But load a large one: more cargo, more gain,
Profit on profit. That is, if squalls refrain.

But if your foolish heart's hell-bent on trade,
And you aim to flee glum hunger and evade
Debt; for you, I'll fathom the sounding sea,
Landlubber though I am, since as for me,
I've never sailed the broad sea on a ship,   650
Not yet, except to Euboea, my one trip,
From Aulis,[52] where, once, waiting in winter's grip,
The Greeks mustered a great host to deploy
From holy Hellas against fair-womaned Troy,
And that is where I crossed to Chalcis once
For the funeral games established by the sons
Of Amphidamas, great of heart. I won, you hear,
With a hymn, and took the tripod by the ear[53]
And offered it to the Muses of Helikon
Right at the spot where they first set me on
The path of clear-voiced song. That's my sum use   660
Of bolted boats. But even so, of Zeus
Aegis-bearer, I'll speak forth his design,
For the Muses taught me song beyond divine.

The time is ripe for sailing the fifty days
Past solstice, summer in its closing phase,
Season of toil. You will not shipwreck then,
Nor will the sea extinguish all your men,

Unless Earth-shaker, Poseidon, is annoyed,
Or Zeus, King of the Gods, wants you destroyed:
In their hands lies fulfilment, good and ill.
670 While breezes are predictable, when still
The sea is harmless, then, with confidence,
You can entrust your swift ship to the winds –
Drag it to the sea, load all your freight.
But sail back home quick as you can – don't wait
For the new wine and autumnal rain, the fast
Onset of winter, South Wind's fearsome blast
That roils the sea, with the thick autumnal rain
Of Zeus, that makes the sea a sea of pain.

In spring's another chance to sail – when figs
Put forth their new leaves from the topmost twigs,
680 The size of crow's feet – that's when first the sea
Is passable, that is spring sailing – me,
I do not recommend it. There's no charm
In a snatched season – you'd scarce flee from harm.
Men do it though, in ignorance of mind –
Money's the breath of life for poor mankind,[54]
But death at sea's a dreadful thing. Have thought
Of all that I proclaim to you: do not
Load hollow ships with your whole livelihood.
690 Keep most aside, a lesser portion's good.
It's terrible to meet a watery fate –
Bad too if loading your cart with too much weight,
You shatter the axle, and you spoil the freight.

Keep measure in your mind. Ripeness is prime
In every undertaking. In due time,
You ought to bring a wife home – and for you
That's thirty, give or take a year or two;

She should be four years into womanhood,
Wed in the fifth, a virgin. Teach her good
And useful ways. Above all, choose a bride   700
From nearby, having searched on every side,
Lest your marriage make your neighbours' mirth.
There's nothing a man gets of greater worth
Than a good wife, but nothing's colder than
A supper-saboteur, who'll sear her man,
Though he be tough, without a frying pan,
One who will serve his old age to him raw.

Keep retribution of the Blessed in awe.
Don't raise a friend to the footing of a brother,
Nor, if you do, be first to wrong the other.
Don't slander for talk's sake. If he starts trouble
In word or deed, mind you to pay back double;   710
However, if he would again be friends,
And if he plans to offer you amends,
Accept. The man who changes friends is base.
Don't let the mind be perjurer of face.

Don't get a name for many guests, or none,
Don't keep low company, nor be the one
To wrangle with high. Don't ever dare to blame
A man for soul-destroying Need – it came
From the everlasting gods. The greatest treasure
Among men is a chary tongue; the pleasure,   720
A tongue that moves in measure. If you say
Evil, then soon worse words will come your way.
Don't be foul-weathered at the crowded feast;
The pleasure's most when shared; the cost is least.

At break of day, you should not ever pour
Bright wine for Zeus and the other gods before
You've washed your hands; they'll turn a deaf ear and
Spit out your prayers. Make sure you do not stand
Facing the sun when you piss. Do not forget:
Go before sunrise, or after the sun has set,
Nor strip down all the way; the nights are owed
730 To the Blessed Ones. Do not piss on the road[55]
Or off it, as you walk. A man who fears
The gods, who knows what's prudent, squats, or nears
The wall of an enclosed yard. Do not show
Your privates smirched with sex next to the glow
Of your home's hearth – avoid this. And do not sow
Offspring after a wake for the deceased,
Ill-omened; rather, after the immortals' feast.
Don't ford on foot an ever-flowing stream
Before you've prayed, and gazed on its white gleam,
And washed your hands in waters sweet, pristine;
740 A man who crosses a river while unclean,
With evil on his hands, will cause offence
To the gods, who'll give him woe in recompense.

At the gods' fine feasts, it is not politic
To prune the five-branched tree, sere from the quick,[56]
With burnished iron. Don't set the serving cup
Above the mixing bowl while men drink up
Their wine, for this brings down a dreadful fate.
Don't leave a house in an unfinished state
Lest a raucous crow should perch on it and caw.[57]
From an unhallowed cauldron, do not draw
Food, or wash from it: woe is foretold.
750 And do not set a boy who's twelve days old

Upon what can't be moved[58] – that's just as bad –
It will unman a man; nor set a lad
Who's twelve months old, the same doom lies in store.
Don't cleanse man's skin where woman's washed before.
This too, for a while, incurs a dismal price.
And when you near a burning sacrifice,
Don't mock the unseen – the god will take it ill.
Don't urinate in streams that flow downhill
To the sea, or springs. To this, be much averse.
And do not void yourself in them – that's worse!

Act thus: eschew the worthless talk of men.   760
Talk's evil – light and easily raised up, then
Hard to bear, hard to put down again;
For once on many tongues, Rumour's abroad,
Nor wholly dies; she too is a kind of god.

Guard well in mind the Days, which come from Zeus,
Advise your slaves in their allotted use.
For overseeing works, the thirtieth's best,
And for dividing rations, folk attest
Who can distinguish truth. For these days come
From Zeus the Counsellor. Here too are some,
The first, the fourth, the seventh, that are hallow   770
(On the Sabbath, Leto gave birth to Apollo[59]
Of the golden sword); the eighth and ninth. Two more
Days of the waxing month are perfect for
Mortal toil – if sheep are to be shorn,
Or you are gathering in the gladsome corn,
The eleventh and twelfth are fine. The twelfth more fair,
That's when the spider, she who floats in air,
Spins webs midday, and the sav*ant* collects[60]
Her hill of grain. A wise woman erects
Her loom that day, embarking on her work.

780 The thirteenth of the month's a day to shirk
Seed sowing; best for bedding plants in earth.
Mid-sixth's quite bad for plants, good for the birth
Of sons, but as for girls, it is instead
A bad day to be born, or to be wed.
Neither is the month's first sixth day held
Fit for the birth of girls; fair, though, to geld
The flock's young billy goats and rams, and then
Good too for fencing folds. And the birth of men,
Those fond of falsehoods, words both sly and cruel,
And whispers. The month's eighth day, as a rule,
790 Is good for gelding boar and roaring bull,
The twelfth day for the mules who bear and drudge.
On the great twentieth, midday, a judge
Is born, a man of deep, dense-woven thought.
The tenth's good for a man-child to be brought
Into the world; for girls, the mid-fourth. And
The mid-fourth's also when to lay your hand
On sheep and shambling longhorns, and the dog
With jagged teeth, the mules that drudge and slog,
To gentle them. But bear in mind to shun
On the fourth of the waxing month and waning one,[61]
Heart-gnawing cares: a day most sanctified.
800 The month's fourth day is when to lead a bride
Under your roof, once you've glimpsed in the air
Good auguries for this task. Fifth days, beware –
The fifth is terrible, a day to loathe,
When the Furies midwifed at the birth of Oath,
Whom Strife bore as a woe to the forsworn.
Mid-seventh, carefully strew the holy corn
Of Demeter on the threshing floor, smooth-worn;
Then carpenters should hew a chamber's lumber,
Or a boat's ship-shape planks, many in number.

The fourth's when to start building narrow ships.
The middle-ninth[62] gets better as it slips   810
To afternoon – the first ninth though is mild
For all – fine to be born, or sow a child,
Male or female; it is a day not ever
Altogether bad. Few know, however,
The month's thrice-ninth is best for certain tasks:
It's the right day for broaching storage casks,
Or yoking ox or mule or fleet-foot horse,
Or drawing a swift ship with its many oars
To the wine-dark sea. Few name things as they are.
On mid-fourth – holiest of days – open a jar.
Few know the twenty-first is best at dawn   820
And worsens as the evening comes on.

These days are gifts to those who dwell on earth –
The rest, haphazard, with no special worth,
Fateless. One praises one day, one, another;
Few know: a day can go from stepmother
To mother. Blessed and rich is he, who's wise
In all these things, who works, and in the eyes
Of the deathless ones is blameless, one who reads
The omens of birds, avoiding all misdeeds.

Notes

1. *two Strifes on the earth*: In his earlier poem, the *Theogony*, Hesiod describes 'Strife' as being a single (negative) entity, the hard-hearted daughter of Night, who herself gives rise to Toil, Forgetfulness, Hunger, Pains, Combats, Battles, Murders, Slaughters, Wrangles, Lies, Disputes, Lawlessness, Recklessness and Oath. This is a major adjustment – he adds another, good, Strife, also daughter of Night, and, importantly, the first-born. (Somehow one assumes Hesiod himself was the elder brother.)

2. *Potter ... bard*: No doubt proverbial, but interestingly embodied in the *Odyssey*, when Odysseus, dressed as a beggar, is pitted against the beggar Arnaeus (see *Od*. 18.17ff.) for the entertainment of the suitors. Also, in the *Odyssey* (*Od*. 17.381–6), we are given a list of four kinds of skilled 'demiourgoi', workers or craftsmen for public hire who might be called to a house or palace for their services: prophets, healers, woodworkers and bards, a quartet of professions that seems to parallel in some ways Hesiod's own list of four. Even in Homer, beggars and bards are purposefully juxtaposed, perhaps because they both would be expected to 'accompany' a feast. Potters were famously competitive – see Note on the Translation.

3. *kings*: 'Basilêes' is a tricky word – sometimes I translate it as 'kings', sometimes as 'judges' – it could also mean 'lords' or 'chiefs' or 'magistrates'. I'd like to say there is rhyme or reason to my method, but sometimes rhyme is

the reason. Interestingly, Zeus, in the *Theogony*, is the opposite of 'gift-guzzling', he is 'gift-giving'. Kings (judges, etc.), too, in the *Theogony* get only compliments.

4. *Mallow ... asphodel*: Mallow and asphodel could be foraged, and were available even if crops failed, asphodel in particular growing abundantly even in poor and over-grazed soil. Asphodel bulbs would be cooked much like potatoes.

5. *But Zeus hid it away, galled in his heart*: Here follows the first telling of 'Pandora's jar' in literature. (It was Erasmus who first made it a box, perhaps conflating it with the story of Psyche and Prosperina.) Pandora is mentioned, though not named, in the previous *Theogony* (570 ff.), and without the jar-full-of-evils story (though she does have a headband decorated with monsters). Note that there is no specific injunction not to open the jar. We know that Prometheus ('Forethought') and Epimetheus ('Afterthought' or 'Hind-sight') are brothers from the *Theogony*. Predictably, Prometheus, the cleverer and better brother, is the elder.

6. *Prometheus' wry art*: The original prank played by Pro-metheus on the gods (and given to us in the *Theogony*) was that he tricked Zeus out of his portion of the sacrifice (the meat and the offal), by offering instead thighbones wrapped in fat. This became the standard form of sacri-fices, conveniently leaving the meat as leftovers to be consumed by the worshippers.

7. *the Cripple*: The lame blacksmith god, Hephaestus.

8. *Affliction ages men quick as you please*: Almost certainly a marginal note that got incorporated into some versions of the text – this is line 19.360 of the *Odyssey*, where it makes more sense.

9. *the jar's huge lid*: The jar here is a *pithos*, a large storage vessel sometimes as tall as a man. *Pithoi* were also used as vessels in the Bronze Age to bury dead children, perhaps because they suggested a womb-like shape.

10. *humanity*: I have dropped the epithet here for men, 'mero-pon', 'having a share in speech'; the phrase means little

more than humanity, *Homo sapiens* (or *Homo eloquens*) –
people who speak being, simply, humans.

11. *Loved by the gods, their sheep crowding the fold*: Poorly
attested line.

12. *spirits*: The word I am translating as 'spirits' is 'daimones' –
from which we get 'demons', but which refers to minor
benign divinities in Hesiod's time, not unlike guardian
angels. Properly, they are the 'portioners', distributing
men's various fortunes. Interestingly, in Plato's *Phaedrus*,
a meditation on inspiration and the Muses, Socrates talks
about his own daemon, but also tells a fable about the
cicadas, who were once people, but in their love for sing-
ing forgot all else and withered into insects. Socrates
whimsically describes the cicadas as watching over man-
kind and reporting back to the Muses regarding who
honours them and who does not. This passage is clearly in
his mind.

13. *Zeus made a fourth one . . . Oedipus's sheep*: The heroes
of Thebes and Troy are the race of Bronze Age men im-
mediately preceding Hesiod's Iron Age. It is worth noting
that the story of the 'Seven Against Thebes' involves two
brothers, Polynices and Eteocles, who are fighting (and
eventually kill each other) over their paternal inheritance –
Oedipus' kingdom of Boeotian Thebes. The flocks of
Oedipus might seem dismissive, but flocks were wealth.
(Cf. Laura Ingalls Wilder's *Farmer Boy*: 'Even those great
barns could not hold all Father's wealth of cows and oxen
and horses and calves and hogs and sheep.')

14. *And others who sailed . . . lovely hair*: Note that the Tro-
jan War is phrased in terms of a (dangerous and relatively
profitless) sea journey.

15. *Away from the gods . . . face*: 173a–e are almost certainly
later interpolations, hence the brackets.

16. *her evil eye*: 'Stygeropis' is perhaps more literally 'loathsome-
faced', but the sense is of having a hateful look, as well as
hateful to look upon, and in Mediterranean cultures, it is
indeed the hateful look of envy that casts the evil eye, and

I think this would have been the understanding here also of ancient readers.

17. *nightingale*: It seems likely that Hesiod means some other songbird than the nightingale here – the ancient Greek word just means 'singer', and nightingales are dull-plumaged, tawny birds without a variegated neck. Hesiod was no city-slicker to be inaccurate in his bird-watching. The poet Panayotis Ioannides helpfully suggests the song thrush, *Turdus philomelos*, which can be seen and heard even in central Athens, is known for its mellifluous song and bears a distinctly speckled throat. I have kept 'nightingale', however, for its literary resonance.

18. *acorn-crowned, and bee-filled, for such folk*: Living on acorns represents a prelapsarian state (see Lucretius 5.939–40, Virgil, *Georgics* 1.8. Ovid, *Fasti* 4.395–402), a Golden Age, as does an abundance of honey. These are foods offered without agricultural labour. On the island of Kea (Zea) now, there is a movement to reclaim acorns (and acorn flour) as a crop.

19. *Noble blood runs through your veins*: The claim that Perses is of divine stock (the family may have claimed descent from some god-sired hero or other) is, of course, as much a compliment to the author as to his dolt of a brother. But it is curious. The Greek here is actually 'descendant of Zeus'. Elsewhere, Perses is reprimanded for getting into quarrels with his betters, so giving him this aristocratic pedigree is somewhat at odds with the situation as it is presented. Is there an element of sarcasm? Or did the family really have some grand, aristocratic claim, perhaps through the ancestors in Aeolian Kyme? Perses ('Destroyer') is the name of a Titan, but not of Zeus' line. In ancient times there was a tradition, probably sprung from this epithet, that Hesiod's father was indeed named Dios (Zeus); this would then be a bit of a sarcastic joke.

20. *Well-crowned Demeter*: I couldn't fit both epithets in here – Demeter is both well-crowned and revered. I hope she forgives me!

21. *takes into his arms ... brother's back*: The proscription against sleeping with a brother's wife doesn't seem a particularly Greek concern compared with other items on this list (not harming a guest or suppliant, for instance) but does put one in mind of Leviticus 20.21: 'And if a man shall take his brother's wife, it is an unclean thing: he hath uncovered his brother's nakedness; they shall be childless.' Of course, Hesiod is particularly concerned with the treachery of brothers.

22. *According to your means, make sacrifice*: According to Xenophon, Socrates approved of this line, arguing that a poor man's sacrifice was as pleasing to the gods as a rich man's. Something of the 'widow's mite' here.

23. *When Atlas' daughters rise*: About 13 May in Hesiod's time.

24. *the Pleiades ... their setting*: Depending on how this is determined, 27 or 30 October.

25. *Naked sow ... harvest naked*: This may not mean stark naked, but rather stripped down, shirtless – as it were, an exhortation to 'roll up your sleeves'. Elsewhere Hesiod expresses superstitious anxieties about exposing oneself to the sun. On the other hand, in classical times, in the Olympics and at other games, it was a hallmark of athletes to compete naked, and there may be a heroic or competitive element to this, farming as 'agon'.

26. *Cut three feet ... cart*: There is a charm in this passage to modern ears, with all the measurements based on human proportions: a cubit is the length from elbow to extended middle finger; a span is the distance from thumb to little finger in an outstretched hand; foot is self-evident; a palm, or hand's-breadth, was 3 inches. Even today, the height of horses is measured in 'hands' – a 'hand' being 4 inches. The foot varied across Greece in ancient times, from 11½ to 13 inches, so our 12 inches is a reasonable approximation. A span was three-quarters of a foot (9 inches, say). All the items are agricultural implements: a large wooden mortar and pestle would be used for

de-husking grains, and a mallet for breaking up clods of earth.

The dimensions and type of the wagon, though, have perplexed commenters for millennia. The word ('hapsis') I translate as felly (four fellies, curved segments, would make the rim of the wheel could also conceivably refer to a solid disk wheel. The cart could have two wheels or four. The axle seems on the long side. Some (A. S. F. Gow, 'The Ancient Plough', *Journal of Hellenic Studies* 34 (1914), pp. 249–75) have suggested the 7 feet could be cut in half for two axles, but that yields a very narrow wagon. (The axle would have stuck out on both sides of the wheel naves.) Another suggestion is that Hesiod could be refer-ring to an axletree – the beam that runs lengthwise down the undercarriage of the cart and in which axles might be set; he clearly means an 'axle' though by the same word in line 693, where he is concerned that overloading a wagon will break the axle. Maybe it is just a wide farm convey-ance, as the measurements would seem to suggest. It is not clear what measurement determines the wagon's 'size'. Ten palms or hand's-breadths (at 3 inches each) would be 2½ feet. This can't refer to the width, given a 7 foot axle, and would make for a ridiculously abbreviated vehicle in terms of length, but is not unreasonable for height off the ground, and about right for wheel size.

If a span is 9 inches, and there are four fellies to a wheel, each at 3 spans, the circumference of the wheel is 108 inches. Divide this by 3.14 (or a better approximation of Pi), and the diameter of the wheel should be 34 inches and a bit. Hesiod gives the wagon measurement as 10 palms or hand's-breadths, so 30 inches. If this measure-ment refers to the diameter of the wheel, Hesiod is only (by our reckoning of the measurements) a bit over 4 inches off, and may in fact have known some rough estimate of Pi.

Hesiod is not suggesting that the farmer build the wagon, only that he cut the wood for it. (Remember that Hesiod says you will need a hundred boards to make one: after line 455.)

Plato, incidentally, touches on the mystery of the wagon as assessed by its many parts in his dialogue the *Theaetetus* (207a–c), where Socrates is discussing the nature of knowledge with the eponymous interlocutor:

Theaetetus: Please could you give me an example, Socrates.
Socrates: I'm thinking of how Hesiod, for instance, says about a wagon, 'There are one hundred timbers to a wagon.' Now, *I* couldn't say what they are, and I don't suppose you could either; we'd be happy, if someone asked us what a wagon is, to be able to reply, 'Wheels, axle, chassis, rails, yoke.'
Theaetetus: Quite.
(Plato, *Theaetetus*, translated by Robin Waterfield (London: Penguin, 1987, 2004), pp. 124–5)

27. *Athena's henchman*: A carpenter/joiner, indeed here arguably a wainwright.
28. *forty-year-old man should follow along*: This would seem to be the hired man mentioned in line 603. His presence might put us in mind of *Odyssey,* Book 11 in the underworld, where the shade of Achilles (the ultimate symbol of a glorious war hero) says, shockingly, 'Could I but live on the earth, I would rather be the hired man of another, some portion-less man with a lean livelihood, than lord it over all the dead and departed' (my translation).
29. *loaf-of-eight*: No one is sure what exactly an 'arton oktablomon' is, here translated 'loaf-of-eight'. It might refer to a loaf of eight parts. Or perhaps it means a bread that has been kneaded or risen eight times. For what it is worth, in modern Greece, particularly in Crete, there is a traditional bread called 'eptazimo' – 'kneaded-seven-times' – often of chick-pea flour, and that is baked into rusks, a good ploughman's lunch.
30. *crane migrating through the cloudy sky*: Cranes migrating south to Africa from Germany currently reach the

Mediterranean in mid- to late October. Combining this with the setting of the Pleiades as another sign for beginning of ploughing, end of October/1 November.

31. *When first the cuckoo cuckoos in the oak*: Late March, early April, perhaps around the spring equinox.

32. *Your swollen foot*: Swollen feet are a symptom of malnutrition, particularly a lack of protein. (This condition is sometimes called kwashiorkor, and afflicts people, particularly children, in famine-struck areas.)

33. *rolling head over heels*: The word 'trochalon' here suggests the man is bent over like a hoop: Cf. Shakespeare, *The Tempest* (Act One, Scene Two, 259–61):

> Hast thou forgot
> The foul witch Sycorax, who with age and envy
> Was grown into a hoop? Hast thou forgot her?

34. *Sans-a-Bone*: Usually considered to be a kenning for the octopus.

35. *Since the sun . . . is slower peeping out*: In winter, according to Hesiod, the sun spends more time among the Africans.

36. *a man on three legs with a broken bac*k: As in the Sphinx's riddle, the three-legged man is an old man with a cane.

37. *stitch skins of firstling kids together*: It's not clear why the goats need to be first-born ('firstling' is a nice English agricultural term fetched out of Tennyson) and some translations give 'new-born'. During carnival season on the island of Skyros, the men wear a traditional costume that involves goat bells, and a mask made of an aborted or miscarried goat (goat herds lose a certain percentage of kids to miscarriage), which fact I leave here for curiosity's sake. First-born kids might have been marked for sacrifice (and thus for meat and leather).

38. *give / A man a little more on which to live*: It isn't entirely clear here whether the man is being put on smaller or larger rations in the wintertime – there's an argument to

go either way. Possibly it means 'more than half his ration' (i.e., still less than his full summertime ration).

39. *nights who are kind*: In the Greek, Hesiod simply refers to the nights by the euphemistic kenning 'the kindly ones'.

40. *Year's end*: Note that the close/beginning of the year is the spring equinox. This is still true in some cultures, as with the Persian New Year (Nowruz).

41. *Sixty winter days ... first appears*: The winter solstice fell on a slightly different date 2,700 years ago, a bit earlier than today: 19/20 December. So sixty days later would correspond to 17 or 18 February.

42. *the swallow, Pandion's child, will wing*: Pandion was an early king of Athens. Pandion's daughter, Philomela, was turned into a swallow. This alludes to the metamorphosis story of Procne, Philomela and Tereus, turned into the nightingale, the swallow and the hoopoe, the last sometimes a hawk, respectively. (In Ovid, however, it is Philomela who is turned into the nightingale, and Procne into the swallow.) Philomela was raped by her brother-in-law, Tereus, who cut out her tongue so she could not accuse him.

43. *harbinger of Spring*: The association of the return of swallows with the spring was proverbial as well as literal: Cf. 'One swallow does not make a spring' (Aristotle, *Nicomachean Ethics* 1098a 16). Traditionally in modern Greece (perhaps a vanishing tradition, but still sometimes learned in school), children welcome the first swallow of spring with carols on 1 March (the 'Helidonismata').

44. *house-hauler*: The snail.

45. *When thistle blooms, and loud Cicada rings*: English speakers tend to think of the cicada's sound as a buzzing or droning noise, but in Greek, the cicada is definitely a singer, and its sound is music (see Plato's *Phaedrus*). The thistle here is the 'golden thistle' (*Scolymus hispanicus*), a relative of the artichoke. On the island of Angistri, in the Saronic, I see this blooming starting in early to mid-June, accompanied by heat and the zithering of cicadas.

46. *Sirius*: Sirius (the Dog Star) rises at around 22 July.

47. *Bibline wine*: No one is quite sure what 'Bibline' wine is – wine from a region so-named in Thrace? Or might it be a reference to far-flung Egypt? Has something happened to the spelling, and does it really refer to wine from Byblos, the most ancient of Phoenician port cities? (Nearby Euboea traded with all sorts of exotic ports.) At any rate, it is clearly a fine variety, worth mentioning as a 'brand name', as it were, and indicative of trade. It would appear that though Hesiod makes his own home-made wine, on some occasions he drinks an imported variety.

48. *when mighty Orion starts to shine*: Around the summer solstice, (then) 22/23 June.

49. *slaves*: The slaves, or serfs, were part of the extended household. The hired man, on the other hand (see lines 441ff.), was free to come and go according to availability of work.

50. *when Dawn with her rosy fingers / Looks on Arcturus*: Around 10 September.

51. *wings*: Probably sails; could be oars, however.

52. *to Euboea, my one trip, / From Aulis*: This is a bit of a geographical joke – this is one of the shortest journeys that can be done by boat in Greece, and does not involve being on the open sea, but crossing the protected bay between Aulis on the Boeotian mainland to Chalcis. Depending on where exactly you reckon the ancient bay of Aulis was, or eighth-century Chalcis, this 'journey' is from just under 2 to just over 3 miles at most. Chalcis itself is then a mile from the mainland; the narrowest point of the Euripus Strait being only about 125 feet. (In the fifth century BCE, as is true now, this strait was simply spanned with a bridge.) Admittedly the currents of the Euripus itself are tricky, famously switching direction four times a day, but the Euboean sailors were expert at navigating it. Considering that his father swept across the whole Aegean in his black ship, this is surely meant to be sarcastically unimpressive.

53. *took the tripod by the ear*: More accurately a 'two-eared', that is, two-handled tripod. I am a bit free here, but it seems right that in a singing contest one should take the tripod by the ear.

54. *Money's the breath of life for poor mankind*: Technically 'money' did not exist in Hesiod's place and time (coins appear not long after in Lydia in the seventh century BCE), but 'money' has stronger poetic resonance and brings the meaning home to us more directly than 'goods', 'property' or 'possessions' here.

55. *730*: I keep the traditional manuscript lineation here (some editors such as West reorder some of these lines) – I think it makes sense as is.

56. *To prune the five-branched tree, sere from the quick*: I.e., don't clip your nails in public – still sound etiquette: 'A man had better ne'er been born / Than have his nails on a Sunday shorn' (Robert Chambers (ed.), *The Book of Days* 2 vols. (London/Edinburgh: W. and R. Chambers, 1869), vol. 1, p. 526).

57. *Lest a raucous crow should perch on it and caw*: John Cuthbert Lawson, in *Modern Greek Folklore and Ancient Greek Religion* (Cambridge: Cambridge University Press, 1910), describes an augury whereby a crow cawing on a rooftop foretold a death (p. 310).

58. *what can't be moved*: Unclear what is meant by this. Some have suggested either tombstones or altars. It is even possible that this is an opaque reference to (and prohibition of) circumcision.

59. *On the Sabbath, Leto gave birth to Apollo*: I have used 'Sabbath' in the next line for 'seventh', since it does seem to have religious connotations here, and Hesiod may even have known something about the seven-day week from the Near East.

60. *the savant collects*: I couldn't resist the pun – the 'clever' or 'provident' one (the 'savant') is of course the ant.

61. *the waxing month and waning one*: Hesiod divides the lunar month into two halves, waxing and waning.

62. *The middle-ninth*: As well as dividing the lunar month into two halves (waxing and waning), Hesiod seems to divide it into three units of nine days, something akin to our week.

Glossary of Proper Names

Amphidamas A (probably historical) king of Chalcis. Plutarch (46–120 CE), Greek historian and essayist from Chaeronea, Boeotia, says Amphidamas died in a sea battle, and distinguished himself in the Lelantine War, which occurred sometime between c.710 and 650 BCE (some scholars place it earlier), between the two major Euboean city-states, Chalcis and Eretria, over the fertile Lelantine plain.

Aphrodite The goddess of love and beauty. According to the *Theogony*, she was born from sea-foam that arose after the castration of Uranus by Kronus. She is the wife of Hephaestus.

Apollo God of prophecy, archery, medicine and the arts, brother of Artemis, son of Leto and leader of the Muses. His seat of worship was on Delos.

Arcturus A bright star easily visible to the naked eye, found in the sky by following the end of the handle of the Plough or Big Dipper (part of the constellation of Ursa Major, the Great Bear). The name in Greek means 'guardian of the bear'. Notably, in *Works and Days* Hesiod is not much interested in mythological stories associated with the stars – they are viewed matter-of-factly, and closely observed, as indicators of the progress of the year.

Askra Hamlet in Boeotia at the foot of Mount Helikon, famous only for Hesiod. Modern Askri (near the site of ancient Askra) is similarly a sleepy agricultural town.

Athena Daughter of Zeus, goddess of wisdom, wiles, weaving and warcraft.

Atlas A Titan, the son of Iapetus and Clymene, and father of the Pleiades. He holds up the sky on his shoulders as he stands near the Hesperides (i.e., in the West).

Aulis Boeotian harbour across from the island of Euboea, the site where the Greek fleet assembled for the expedition against Troy, and the site traditionally of the sacrifice of Iphigenia when the fleet was becalmed. It was well suited for a large muster of ships, lying directly across the bay from well-wooded Euboea (for ship-building timber), having deep water, and being protected from storms.

Cadmus Legendary prince of Phoenicia (or sometimes Egyptian Thebes), who came to Greece in search of his sister, Europa. He initially settled in Thrace, but obeyed an oracle at Delphi that he was to follow a sacred cow until it should lie down, and build a city on the spot. In this way, he founded the city of Thebes in Boeotia. He is said to have introduced an early alphabet of sixteen letters from the Phoenicians, sometimes called the 'Cadmean Letters'.

Chalcis The principal town of the island of Euboea (3 miles to the north of Aulis across the Euripus Strait), which in Hesiod's time and earlier was a flourishing centre of trade, and spearheaded Greek settlements in Sicily and Italy.

Demeter Goddess of the earth and agriculture (thus sometimes simply representing the earth), and one of the twelve Olympian gods. She is the daughter (in the *Theogony*) of Kronos and Rhea, and sister to Hades, Poseidon, Hera, Hestia and Zeus.

Dionysus God of the grape harvest, wine and drama, thus sometimes (as here) simply standing in for wine. In mythology, he is the son of Zeus and the mortal princess Semele, herself the daughter of Cadmus (founder of Thebes). (His bloodline is thus both divine and Boeotian.)

Euboea 'Well Cattled', the largest island in the Aegean (and of the Greek islands, only Crete is larger), about 90 miles in length, lying mostly along Boeotia, separated by a bay from the mainland, and, at its narrowest, the Euripus Strait. It was an active centre of trade-routes all across the Mediterranean, flourishing during the 'Dark Ages', especially at the site of Lefkandi, when many other Greek settlements were in decline. Euboea had two main city-states, Chalcis and Eretria.

Epimetheus The name means 'afterthought'; the brother of the Titan Prometheus and husband of Pandora, the first woman.

Graces According to Hesiod, daughters of Zeus and Eurynome. They are the three goddesses of loveliness, joy and charm.

Helikon Mountain (actually a mountain range) in the far west of Boeotia overlooking Boeotia to the east and the Gulf of Corinth to the west. In later literature it is identified with the Muses and inspiration generally, home to the sacred springs of inspiration, the Aganippe and the Hippocrene, 'Horse Spring'. (Remember Keats's 'Ode to a Nightingale': 'O for a beaker full of the warm South, / Full of the true, the blushful Hippocrene').

Hephaestus The god of smiths, craftsmen and artisans, Hephaestus is the son of Hera. (He has no father, according to the *Theogony*; Hera bore him out of spite.) Lamed after being hurled from Olympus, he is wedded to Aphrodite, goddess of love and beauty.

Hermes Messenger of the gods, often called the 'killer of Args'. Args was a famous monster, though there are other theories on the meaning of his epithet 'argeiphontes': 'dog-slayer', perhaps, or 'brightly shining'.

Hours The Seasons, they are the daughters of Zeus and Themis. Among their other sisters are Order, Justice, Peace and the Fates.

Hyades A cluster of stars located in Taurus. In Greek their name may mean 'the rainy ones'. They were supposed to be daughters of Atlas.

Iapetus According to the *Theogony*, a Titan, son of Uranus and Gaia (Sky and Earth), and father of Atlas, Prometheus, Epimetheus and Menoetius.

Kronos Son of Uranus and Gaia (Earth and Sky), father of Zeus, Hera, Hades, Hestia, Demeter and Poseidon. He ate his children because of a prophecy that his sons would overpower him, as he had overthrown his own father, Uranus. His wife and sister, Rhea, tricked him when Zeus was born, giving him a rock to swallow instead, and hiding Zeus to grow up in safety. Zeus later freed his brothers and sisters. Kronos presided over a golden age.

Kyme (Aeolian) Greek settlement in Asia Minor (modern Turkey) on the coast near to the island of Lesbos. Hesiod's father hailed from Aeolian Kyme.

Lenaion Only here does Hesiod use the name of a month (elsewhere he refers to the time of year by signs in nature). The names of the months varied across Greece; curiously, the month is an Ionian, not a Boeotian, one. (Nearby Euboea did observe the Ionian calendar.) It corresponds roughly to the period between mid-January and mid-February, a time that can be very cold in Greece.

Leto In the *Theogony*, Hesiod describes Leto as the daughter of the Titans Coeus and Phoebe. By Zeus, she becomes the mother of the twin divinities Apollo and Artemis. She is a goddess of motherhood, so her bringing forth of Apollo on the seventh day would make it especially propitious. The special importance of the seventh day may have been imported under Babylonian and Semitic influence (hence my use of the religiously loaded word 'Sabbath').

Muses The nine goddesses of inspiration, they are the daughters of Zeus and Mnemosyne (Memory). Hesiod gives their names as Kleio (Fame Maker), Euterpe (Well-Delighting), Thaleia (Blooming), Melpomene (Singer), Terpsichore (Delighting in Dance), Erato (Lovely), Polymnia (Much Hymning), Ourania (Heavenly) and Kalliope (Lovely Voiced). Later antiquity gave each Muse a specific sphere of influence (history, song, pastoral, tragedy, etc.) and attribute.

Oedipus 'He of the Swollen Foot'. Legendary king of Thebes, whose story is best known from the Theban plays of Sophocles. Because of a prophecy that he would kill his father and marry his mother, he was exposed as a baby, but adopted by the king and queen of Corinth. He later did kill his birth father (King Laius) at the crossroads, and married his widowed mother (Jocasta) by accident, after gaining the empty throne by guessing the riddle of the Sphinx. Oedipus cursed his two sons, Eteocles and Polynices, by giving them joint leadership over his kingdom when he departed it. (They were supposed to fight it out.) They tried to get around the curse by alternating rule annually, but when Eteocles refused to cede the throne, Polynices brought an army against him, thus triggering the war of Seven Against Thebes, in which both brothers were slain.

Orion One of the most recognizable constellations, located on the celestial equator. In mythology, Orion was a giant and hunter (born, coincidentally, in Boeotia). Again, Hesiod is not concerned with the constellation as mythology, but only as an indicator of the seasons.

Pandion Legendary king of Athens, and father of Procne and Philomela, who were turned into a nightingale and a swallow respectively (Ovid inverts this).

Pandora The 'All-endowed', 'All-gifted', the first woman according to Greek mythology, given by the gods to mankind as a punishment for Prometheus' theft of fire.

Perses Perses is Hesiod's brother (and I would assume younger brother), involved in a lawsuit with Hesiod over their inheritance. The name itself would seem to mean something like 'destroyer' or even 'wastrel'.

Pieria The region in Greece where Mount Olympus is located, home of the sacred spring of the Muses. (Remember Alexander Pope: 'A little learning is a dang'rous thing; / Drink deep, or taste not the Pierian spring.')

Pleiades A cluster of six visible stars, sometimes known as the 'Seven Sisters', located in Taurus. (Just look at the logo of Subaru, and you will see their distinctive pattern.) In mythology, they were seven nymphs, daughters of Atlas.

Poseidon Son of Kronus and Rhea, and brother of Zeus, he is the god of earthquakes, horses and the sea.

Prometheus Son of the Titan Iapetus and Clymene. His brothers were Atlas, Menoetius and Epimetheus. His name means 'forethought' (in fact, in modern Greek it is the word for 'provisions'), and he was renowned for cleverness, though this got him in trouble with the gods. He tricked Zeus out of his share of a sacrifice, and was chained to a rock, where an eagle tore at his liver every day (it grew back each night). He was rescued by Heracles (Hercules), a Boeotian hero. Having stolen fire from the gods, he incurred the punishment of the first woman, Pandora, and the hiding of livelihood, necessitating work. Pandora, however, was given to his brother, Epimetheus.

Sirius The brightest star in the night sky, sometimes known in English as the 'Dog Star'. The name in Greek means 'scorcher' and the star's rising was associated with the heat wave of late summer.

Thebes The principal city of Boeotia; in legend, founded by Cadmus, and associated with the hero Heracles (Hercules). The alphabet was said to have been introduced from Phoenicia into Western Europe here. It was here the mythological tragedy of Oedipus unfolded, and consequently the battle of the Seven Against Thebes over Oedipus' legacy.

Thrace An area in and beyond north-eastern Greece of uncertain extent, noted for its wildness and horses.

Troy City in Asia Minor (modern Turkey), the site of the legendary Trojan War, the expedition of Greeks to take back Helen, wife of Menelaus, who had been spirited away by the Trojan prince Paris.

Zeus Supreme ruler of the gods on Olympus, the son of Rhea and Kronos. Justice, law and order, as well as the authority of kings, are in his purview. A sky god, his attributes are the lightning bolt and thunder. He is the father of any number of gods, heroes and goddesses, including the nine Muses.